BEHIND
SHADES

MARÍA BIRD PICÓ

# BEHIND SHADES

Translated by
*Melba Ferrer*

PUBLICACIONES
TE PIENSO

*To Tere,*
*the one and only underneath María's*
*complicated shades.*

*To Juan Andrés and Ana Carolina,*
*the brightest stars behind my shades.*

*To my medio mangó,*
*for shining light.*

# INDEX

## SUBVERSIVE WOMEN WEAR SUNGLASSES: MARÍA BIRD PICÓ'S BEHIND SHADES

By Ivonne M. García, Ph.D., The College of Wooster

In the final story of the fifteen-tale collection titled Behind Shades by María Bird Picó, translated into English by Melba Ferrer, the protagonist, Linda (a.k.a. "La Güima"), is an overweight, fifty-something band singer, with more enthusiasm than talent. Her nickname, which means "the guinea pig," reflects "an overbite of crooked teeth never tamed by orthodontics." Linda, however, likes to think that the nickname means "that, in life, she has been her own guinea pig, testing the boundaries of what might be thought ordinary." And test the boundaries she does, like all other protagonists in this collection of stories. This last tale, aptly titled "The Formula," neatly summarizes the collection's own recipe: the refusal to be tamed and to be ordinary by a cast of sensual, passionate, initially culturally-conforming women characters, who find themselves extraordinarily altered—often in real-magical ways (and here I use the literal translation of the real mágico)—after subverting societal/cultural expectations.

The sunglasses—the "shades" of the title—function as both a recurring symbol throughout the stories and as main trope for the empowerment that these women achieve when shading, or occluding, their more conventional, conforming selves. The metaphor also serves as a metonym for how gender norms shade, or distort, not only the way these ambitious, driven women are perceived by others, but also how they perceive themselves. In La Güima's case, it is only after an annoyed spectator, tired of Linda's poor singing, hurls a pair of sunglasses at the singer and Linda puts them on (even though it's nighttime), that the audience members "suddenly see wonder, promise, power, mystery, talent" where they had seen none of these before.

With short, mostly one-word titles that reflect emotional states ("Illusion," "Vulnerability," "Irreverence," "Bliss," "Essence," "Achilles' heel,"), goals ("Perfection," "Duty," "Habit," "Liberation," "Fame"), and life-changing moments ("The Encounter," "The Challenge," The Formula"), Bird Picó appears to set the tone for the *moraleja*, the lesson, we are to take from the story. But then, just like the collection itself, the stories turn against and away from easy resolutions as morality or cautionary tales. In most of the stories, the women characters move from passive observers to purposeful actors, even when they don't understand why or what (in a kind of madness) they are doing. In "Illusion," 27 years after a torrid dalliance, a woman and a man make a pact to meet at the Plaza de Mayo but then fail to recognize each other, mostly because they have aged in unflattering ways and both are still expecting to meet their younger selves. Self-delusion, concerns over body shape and image, and the illusive power of unfulfilled expectations are running themes through many of the stories, as is the battle between desire and self-control, between concealing and revealing. These stories aren't about women satisfied with their roles as mothers and wives, but about women who want to break free from the fetters of their respective worlds.

One of the most accomplished stories along those lines is "Fame," a twisted fairy tale, reminiscent of Nathaniel Hawthorne's "The Birthmark" and of Oscar Wilde's The Picture of Dorian Gray, but with a definite feminist perspective. In this story, a gorgeous model, Catalina, gives birth to "a beautiful baby, with fresh, rosy skin." But in the exact moment that the baby is born, Catalina begins to grow horrible warts all over her face and for every pound the baby gains, she gains six, ending up with almost 100 extra pounds. While large sunglasses help her hide "the tubers on her right cheek," and Catalina begins to hide "her ample figure under a gypsy tunic," she feels cursed and even her husband, Esteban, believes "the baby had hexed her mother." Catalina, however, eventually accepts "her condition and her new body," acquiring "a taste for wide tunics," and "dabbing on bright colors [on her warts], making them appear as if they were stray moons in a newborn galaxy." She takes her bodily changes as "Heaven [...] testing" her, and begins "to truly enjoy being with her baby," forgetting "the conviction that she had been hexed."

However, this story is unlike the fairy tales in which the frog or beast is restored into a handsome prince, or in which, as in Hawthorne's tale, the wife is appalled by the birthmark that, when finally removed by her husband to grant her absolute perfection, actually kills her. Bird Picó does craft a story in which motherhood exacts its usual price on a woman's body: the gained weight and the forever altered perception, not only by others but also by the self. But, instead of remaining in a state in which the monstrous changes are perceived as horrid, Catalina accepts her newly reconfigured body and face, and learns to love her child despite the devastation maternity has caused in her previously idealized and culturally-conforming being. When the real magic intercedes (as it does in other stories), and Catalina achieves fame again—not for being perfect but for being perfectly content with her monstrously reconfigured self—she is returned to her original shape. Here, again, Bird Picó subverts the genre's expectations by giving us a Catalina that prefers herself in the version that society has interpreted as monstrous, and vows that she will "be beautiful again" in the terms she has constructed for herself, not because she meets societal-cultural expectations of beauty. This is perhaps one of the most subversive of the stories in the collection, and in contrast to Carmen Maria Machado's *Her Body and Other Parties*, which also reworks fairy tales to point to the many troubling and troubled ways in which women are constrained and limited, Bird Picó ends this fantasy with a message of present and future empowerment. Catalina rebels not by rejecting or fighting against the negative events in her life but by taking control of her own story and telling it in her own—rather than in society's, the patriarchy's, or the culture's—terms.

Ultimately, the transformative, if dangerous power of change in and for women is the thru-theme in this collection. However, as I've pointed out, these aren't simplistic fairy tales or *telenovelas* that end with traditional happily-ever-afters. Some stories end ambiguously, in ways that make us wonder what Bird Picó means to say (and perhaps we are meant to feel baffled and disturbed rather than enlightened). But the author defines her characters so precisely and convincingly that each protagonist comes to life, becoming unforgettable and its own case study. Bird Picó's women always have something to hide or something that isn't obvious to themselves and/or to everyone else. By hiding behind sunglasses, her protagonists all ask us to look, to inquire: what's being concealed and why? What appears to be evident but isn't? The often successful, cosmopolitan, sensual women in Bird Picó's globally situated stories are often at war with themselves, whether with their weight, their sexual desires, their life choices, and always in conflict with the domesticity that wants to cage them in traditional roles. These are all women with talent, intelligence, and grit, who face particular challenges that define them, even as it leads many of them to madness or to an unresolved stasis. By the end, we find pieces of ourselves in many of Bird Picó's protagonists, and like all great fairy tales and *telenovelas*, her stories remind us that there is a price to be paid for the choices we make. But also, and unlike the genres that her collection both adapts and challenges, her stories call on us to understand that freedom is power, and that women are always-already powerful, even if they can't see it for themselves, especially because while they may still be wearing shades, they're no longer hiding behind them.

# ILLUSION

Rosana Guzmán arrived at Plaza de Mayo ten minutes before the appointed hour. She sat on a bench, taking extra care not to wrinkle her red dress. The moment she had awaited for twenty-seven years had finally arrived: she would finally see her beloved Mauricio.

Rosana used the remaining minutes for touching up her lipstick and brushing her short hair, now impeccably dyed black. She also made sure her designer sunglasses were carefully in place. She felt in control and satisfied because she had resisted the temptation to pop a pill to calm her nerves. In her red Louis Vuitton bag was a newspaper clipping on *The Encounter*, the play written by Mauricio García, the man she had loved since the two were in college. She also carried her only picture of them together. In it was a thin girl with a shy smile, an attempt to focus attention away from the thick glasses covering her face. Next to her was Mauricio, with his fit physique and eternal tan, wearing his customary T-shirt and a pair of jeans accented by a wide, rustic leather belt.

She remembered how all the gringo girls in college would go crazy over Mauricio's black mane and his macho demeanor. He was handsome and gentle, and campus rumors had it that he would serenade his girlfriend *du jour* with his guitar, which was tattooed in quotes by Simón Bolívar and Che Guevara, and how they would make love by candlelight to the music of Sandro. She had asked Mauricio for a picture of them together on the last day of their Latin American History course in college. He agreed, and why not? For a whole year, the two had pored over books on Perón, Árbenz, Allende, and Caribbean colonialism. It was during those evenings, immersed in the music of Pablo Milanés, Silvio Rodríguez and Atahualpa Yupanqui, that Rosana fell in love with Mauricio, imbibing his aroma, his passion for literature, and his habit of taking three slow deliberate puffs of his cigarette before answering a question. He had no idea how much she was in love with him, nor could he even imagine the sparks that ran through her body every time he brushed his arm against hers as when he reached for a book. If Rosana was not worthy of his love, compared to the dazzling and frisky blonds surrounding him, at least she would have the memories of those college sessions together. Her passion for Mauricio continued throughout the years, the decades, and did not waver even through her marriage and her many ensuing lovers.

Rosana was still amazed at her courage when she called Teatro Solís in Montevideo to inquire as to the whereabouts of Mauricio, whose play was being staged there. She only had to mention her name -Rosana Guzmán- to get his phone number. Twice she dialed his number in Buenos Aires, and twice she hung up when she heard his voice. She called a third time and managed to whisper "Mauricio." She was surprised at how he immediately recognized her voice.

The conversation quickly began to flow. After all, Rosana, now accustomed to success and her many book signings, had long overcome her shyness. Thanks to her writer's discipline and dogged persistence, she had made a name for herself among Latin America's intellectual circles. A French filmmaker had even directed her award-winning novel, *Lover for Sale.* Her first three novels, previously ignored, were now sold out. It didn't matter that the first two were romance novels about guerrilla fighters.

"When I read *Lover for Sale* I longed to see you again, but I didn't know where to find you," Mauricio told her.

"I felt the same way when I read *The Encounter.* I'm calling because I'm in Uruguay and I'll be going to Buenos Aires next week to visit some friends." She lied, not wanting Mauricio to know she was traveling there just to see him.

A honk from a nearby bus brought Rosana back to her sullen reality, sans Mauricio. Once back from her trip into the past, Rosana looked around. She again checked her mirror, making sure that her lips hadn't lost their seductiveness, that her four-inch-high red stilettos were shiny, and that her pantyhose had not sprung a last-minute run.

***

Mauricio García tried in vain to light his fifth cigarette that morning. Every three minutes he made another attempt at this simple task, but his trembling hands simply would not allow it. He was five minutes late, after a torturous moment of sheer cowardice. He scanned the square, but saw no signs of his Rosana amid the morning crowd.

He leaned against the statue of a forgotten statesman, searching the pockets of his old coat for a worn copy of *Lover for Sale*. Rosana remained every bit as mysterious as in the past; there was no photo of her on the back cover. Mauricio imagined her looking the same as the last time he'd seen her: devoid of makeup, and with long hair now with some grey, overshadowing her librarian's glasses. She would probably still be wearing a long, flowing maxi skirt and a hippie-like cotton shirt. Her small feet would be wrapped in leather sandals. If she only knew how much he had thought about her all these years, and how he had longed to sit next to her and discuss world politics and culture as they had so many times before.

He remembered how Rosana loved politics, and how she knew the story of every Latin American guerilla movement. She could spend hours talking about the Tupamaros, Sandino, and the Montoneros. She knew Castro's and Allende's key speeches by heart. Mauricio remembered the many times he had casually brushed his arm against hers, attempting to elicit a reaction, but Rosana never, ever, responded. He never dared kiss her, either, intimidated by that mixture of brilliance, naiveté, intellectual ebullience, and shyness. None of his lovers, each more daring and outlandish than the one before, were ever able to quell his desire for Rosana, a desire that compelled him to write *The Encounter*.

He drew three consecutive puffs from the cigarette, which was now disappearing from his fingers, and then tapped his old wristwatch, attempting to revive it. It was ten thirty-eight, and no sign of Rosana.

And to think that he had lied when he told her he was cancelling another date to see her, when in fact he'd spend days drinking and reminiscing about better times. He hadn't written anything in years, living off the success and scant royalties from his only two plays, which were now included in school curricula. His wife Laura and his two children had left him three years earlier, when he was arrested for walking naked through the streets, carrying a lit candle and singing Sandro songs. The desire to see Rosana once again had kept him sober throughout this week, and he'd even dropped a kilo or two from the many he had gained since he had stopped writing. He was excited now, and had begun to write a play that he was thinking of calling *Vintage Love.* He was going to show Rosana the first few pages. Brushing back grey strands of hair, Mauricio tapped his watch again and pulled out his sixth cigarette.

***

For the twelfth time, Rosana looked at her watch. It was ten-forty, and no sign of her Mauricio. She imagined him naked next to an adoring young college girl, exhausted by so much lovemaking. She shot up, furious at herself for having given in, after nearly thirty years of dreaming about and desiring him. And to think that, judging from the phone call, she had actually believed that Mauricio wanted to see her again.

Holding back the tears, Rosana stormed out of the square and bumped into a fat, balding man who reeked of sweat and cigarettes. She swore. The man dropped a book. Rosana saw that it was a copy of *Lover for Sale*, and she hurried away, fearing that this scruffy lowlife might ask her for an autograph.

***

As he recovered his balance, Mauricio shot acrid words at the fleeing woman in red. He picked up his copy of *Lover for Sale,* mumbling to himself how foolish he had been for even thinking that his luck had changed after twenty-seven years. He dropped the book and his manuscript in the nearest trash can and, once again, sought comfort in a welcoming bottle.

# VULNERABILITY

Regina Leal assessed the imminent danger when she saw the crowd. The protest was taking place in front of the Capitol. Were it not for the changing messages on the banners—the cooking pots were always the same, hard and worn—today's demonstration would have been just another one. Some of the faces were even the same, protest after protest, which made her wonder more than once whether picketing had become a new line of work.

Regina pulled out a handkerchief from the pocket of her tight police uniform pants and wiped her brow, without removing her customary sunglasses. She smiled thinking about the time the chief of police had tried to ban the wearing of sunglasses while on duty, but his order was disregarded after rising acerbic public outcries, sabotaged telephone lines and workers' strikes.

As she observed the crowd of protesters, Regina began to remember how she became a cop. As a child, she had watched in awe televised images from England of the Queen's Guard. She would wonder how the guards, crowned by bearskin caps, managed to remain rigid for so many hours. She was fascinated by the possibility that they might be imagining stories, devising new scientific or existential theories, or musing about life, while thousands of tourists and passersby remained oblivious to the complexity contained within that solitude.

Now, along with thirty other officers stationed at the barricade, Regina was keeping the demonstrators at bay. The police had orders to maintain the crowd at a distance from the stairway leading to the Capitol building's main entryway.

The day's heat, the sudden rain, the government's indifferent attitude, the tightness of the police barricade and the heated atmosphere were announcing danger. Yet, with so many workers' strikes under her belt, Regina remained unfazed. Throughout the past three decades, she had earned the respect of the other officers after many hours of service in which she, despite her small frame, remained courageous and impassive. She wore no makeup, only a hint of red on her fleshy lips. Her co-workers often kidded her, saying that the touch of red helped confuse assailants who were not expecting a detail like that on a woman with such a menacing figure. Regina always tied her frizzy hair in a ponytail that hid part of a scar starting behind her cheek and ending at the nape of her neck. Her photo, with her bloodied but expressionless face hidden by sunglasses, had made the front pages.

From the corner of her eye, she kept noticing the young student who angrily shook a stick and raised her right fist. Next to her, a sixty-something woman was struggling to keep time, as she beat a pot with a large spoon. Regina watched her closely, keeping in mind that it was increasingly common for people in their sixties to engage in violence.

Had she wanted to, Regina could have worked in any division of the Police Department. She had been awarded many honors for her exemplary service, and her cool demeanor had been the subject of several newspaper stories. But what she really enjoyed was the sense of power she felt in these demonstrations, during which she remained standing for hours, undaunted by the jeers, the insults, and even the flirtatious remarks from the crowds. She felt at peace being able, like the English guards, to bring order, simply through her self-control, namely when her kaleidoscope eyes were hidden behind shades. Her mother would often say that, even as a baby, Regina's eyes were so revealing that one could tell what she was thinking or feeling just by glancing at them. Many were the tales of how she was unable to mask her feelings because her eyes would give her away. Edgardo, her first love at the age of fifteen, knew that she was lying when she batted her eyelids, all the while saying that she wanted to end the relationship because she had no time for a commitment.

"That's a downright lie," he said. "You're seeing someone else."

From that day on, she guarded her weaknesses, joys and sorrows behind sunglasses. At the age of forty, she felt even more vulnerable and hid behind darker shades.

Regina placed her right hand over her ear to adjust the earphone that conveyed her orders.

"Don't loose sight of the white kid with the green eyes," said the voice on the radio. It was the sergeant, who secretly kept close tabs on the scene. "He was the one who hit officer López during the protest against the tax on sanitary napkins."

Regina turned her head toward the young man, whose green eyes made him easy to spot. He looked at her defiantly for a few seconds, but then lowered his gaze. Regina congratulated herself. Once again, she did not even have to lift a finger to keep order.

"Leal, ready. Someone is closing in from the right," said the voice over the radio. "Don't let appearances fool you."

Without moving her head at all, Regina was able to examine a white-haired woman who looked as if she could easily be a great-grandmother. She was coming closer, slowly but surely, with the help of a cane. The woman's eyes shone with an anger that spewed over her wrinkled visage and made her even more ferocious-looking.

"You!" cried the woman, pointing to Regina. "You should be ashamed of yourself!" Although she remained emotionless, Regina's body stiffened, while her thoughts continued their rambling course. She imagined at that moment what her three-year-old grandson Antonio might be up to. Had he eaten the lemon pie she had sent him? Had they told him that granny had made it just for him?

"Bitch!" yelled the woman as she came closer, holding her cane in the air. "Pig!"

Regina then turned her attention to last night's episode of the Mexican *telenovela*, *Love on Reins*. Would Alicia finally give in to Armando? Would she sign the waiver and do away with her right to have children? How would Alicia's mother react to the fact that she would never become a grandmother?

"Traitor!" cried the woman, just inches from Regina's face. "You are a disgrace to all women!"

Regina's otherwise cold blood began to boil. For decades she had heard all sorts of insults, but something in that woman's tone irked her. Nevertheless, her self-control immediately kicked in and her thoughts clung to her small grandson and the pie that she had so lovingly baked using fresh lemons from the only fruit-bearing tree left standing in her yard after the hurricane. Using fresh eggs was the key to a fluffy meringue. This time, she did not frost the pie, so that she would not have to hear her daughter-in-law's never-ending litany of how kids today eat way too much sugar.

"Leal, to your left, more are approaching with canes and walkers," blared the radio. "*You* are the target."

Regina's thoughts went back to the handsome Armando of *Love on Reins*. He was a romantic, compassionate, caring gentleman—any woman's dream. Why wouldn't he want to have children? Would he change his mind when he approached old age? Would he demand that Alicia have her tubes tied to avoid pregnancy?

Adrenaline turned to fuel when Regina saw that the advancing army was truly a band of women pretending to be white-haired little old ladies with canes and walk-

ers. She curbed her mounting outrage by remembering
the first time she'd held her grandson on her lap. That
was the moment when she swore she would set aside
one day each week for pampering him. Little Antonio
first tasted her lemon pie when he was fourteen months
old. His eyes lit up and he uttered his very first "Nanny."

Tears welled in Regina's eyes, but her shades made
her feel protected.

"Leal, keep still. They are provoking you," ordered
the radio.

She never knew where the blow that sent her sunglasses hurtling into the crowd came from. Regina
blinked while the mob insulted her. The sun's rays
added injury to insult. She felt the need to close her
eyes, fearing what they would reveal to the enemy, but
her discipline once again took over. She needed to keep
a level head and know what the crowd was doing at
every moment. Two of the hecklers approached and
began to gesticulate near her face. Regina kept her cool,
attempting to return to her thoughts of lemon pie and
handsome, but fickle, actors.

"Leal, we are ready to rescue you," said the voice.
"Congratulations for a job well done, as always."

Eva, the protestors' leader, pulled off her white wig,
threw the cane aside, approached Regina and stared at
her. A hush overtook the usually noisy crowd. Regina's
eyes revealed a sour combination of hurt and happiness.
She could not help but think of her grandson, as well
as the challenges that Alicia and Armando would have
to overcome. Would Alicia demand alimony in case of
a divorce? Regina imagined her grandson running to
the kitchen for a slice of pie. Would they allow him to

eat it from the pie dish, or would they make him wait until the slice was properly served on a plate? Would Alicia's mother adopt a child if Alicia signed the waiver?

For Regina, it was hard to acknowledge that reality was still staring her in the face. Eva's eyes revealed revenge.

Regina wanted to disappear, but, alas, that was not possible. She did not move an inch. She tried to go back to lemons, fresh eggs, flour, her grandson. To no avail. Trying to remember how Alicia was dressed in last night's episode and the synopsis of this night's episode didn't help much, either.

A woman holding a pot in one hand and a cane in the other moved in closer, with the intention of burying Regina with her hatred. She glared at Regina, straight in the naked eye, but Eva stopped her. Amid the incredulous gaze of her followers, Eva signaled a retreat. Regina remained still, cursing the moment. Bewildered, the protestors began to abandon the area. Once the very last one had gone, the other officers started leaving, without looking back at their companion. Regina stayed behind, majestic and proud, the champion of the event.

"Good work, Leal," said the radio. "You have permission to leave." But Regina remained in place, trying to recall the images of her grandson, of Alicia and Armando, of the lemon pie. She would not move until two hours later, when an approaching passerby recognized her and covered her eyes with a pair of sunglasses.

# IRREVERENCE

The conversation over the blue gingham tablecloth turns to politics. As usual, Roberto Santos Patín has a lot to say. If there is something that incites him, it's politics and how it affects society, individuals, and the economy. Roberto puffs out his chest and expands his five-foot-ten-inch frame, seeming as though he had rehearsed his speech for hours before finally arriving with his shy and proper wife, Celeste, at the provincial *Sin Censura* pub for the monthly get-together of the lawyers from the firm.

Roberto takes a two-ounce gulp of tequila, smacks his lips, and opens his mouth to show two perfectly aligned rows of immaculate teeth.

"Totalitarian systems do work," he affirms. "The problem is that their leaders have failed because they rely on obsolete theories."

His words have the desired effect; everyone at the table turns their attention to him and gives him coaxing looks. Roberto ties back his graying mane with the worn red-and-white scarf that only seconds ago was his necktie. It is a well-known gesture, signaling unequivocally that Roberto is only getting started.

During the short pause, which includes summoning the waiter for another round of tequilas, all those gathered at the table dig in and devour the last pieces of *morcilla* blood sausage which, with their last ounce of dignity, await being pierced by toothpicks. One piece covered in a whitish layer of fat is left on the platter, urging any brave person to finish the task.

Only one person notices the solitary sausage's beckoning: the timid Celeste. She finds it funny that the very same people who only six minutes earlier could not hide their voracious appetites were now ignoring the lone piece of *morcilla*.

She entertains herself by thinking that the tavern falls short of its efforts at refinement by serving such unsophisticated delicacies. Not even the pink blown-glass plate or the pastel-colored scented candles on the table are able to disguise the lowly sausage's coarse appearance.

Not that it is ugly. As a matter of fact, it is well shaped, with its centuries-old heritage enclosed in a smooth casing. Its color is perfect: black with a showering of white specks, denoting great care in its crafting. From its black mouth spring eight little white dots, a sufficient amount which, according to the menu, gives it a distinction in the International Society of *Morcilla* Chefs.

After some thought, Celeste concludes that the reason why this piece was left behind is that the order contained thirteen pieces. She again wonders why restaurants have the habit of serving uneven orders in which a piece is always left over. Pizzerias, for example, insist on saying that a regular pie yields eight slices. But she has proven, with no doubt whatsoever, that some pies yield nine slices, and others yield only seven. She has finally desisted calling the managers to complain because they all react in the same way: "Ma'am, it's still the same amount of pizza, regardless of how many slices."

Celeste looks around the table in search of the brave soul who will devour the last *morcilla* standing. She is sure that José Ernesto Cintrón Rivera, the glutton of the group, will save face by not succumbing to this bit of temptation. All of his friends surmise that he pigs out in private—which may explain why his girth continues to spread out— while out in public he orders salads and seared chicken breasts. His demeanor is the same at work. He seems to be in complete control, while, in fact, he sneaks all his case files home to bone up on his court cases the night before they are due. The dark circles under his eyes are as large as his belly.

Seated next to him, Carmen Rosín Pérez Pinzón excuses herself for the third time to go the restroom. Celeste carefully observed her when she'd first entered the bar, and saw her take three toothpicks from the front desk and place them in her Dior purse. Carmen Rosín simply refuses to pick the black *morcilla* particles encrusted in her teeth in public. As she walks to the restroom, she is followed by ogling eyes, admiring her panty-hosed hips swaying exuberantly on three-inch heels. No, Carmen Rosín will definitely not lay claim to the last *morcilla*. The third and last toothpick in her bag has the sole purpose of cleaning her exquisite smile.

Celeste chuckles, recalling that Carmen Rosín was the only member of the group who was against the idea of eating *Criollo* food. Her husband Alberto convinced her to come along, saying that they also served roasted chicken at the pub. Needless to say, despite being so finicky, Carmen Rosín had joined her friends in devouring steaming bowls of pigs' feet in sauce, with the excuse that she did not want to seem too demanding and that, for Christ's sake, children in Africa are going hungry. For her second helping, she wiped away an imaginary tear and said: "Those poor kids in Haiti are dying of hunger and we continue to throw away food."

What about Alberto Torres Bryan? Would he dare eat the lone *morcilla*? Not a chance. He blindly follows Carmen Rosín's orders. Roberto's theory is that, with such a knockout of a woman, Alberto has no need to express himself. Besides, Celeste thinks, Alberto doesn't eat all that much. Proving her theory is the fact that Alberto has been using the same Colombian leather belt for years, with a 32-inch waist. But what makes him the most productive member of the law firm is his strict work ethic. In fact, he is the only member of the firm who abides by the rule to not discuss personal matters at business luncheons, considering such topics superficial.

"But there is no reason for the economy to be in such a slump," says Roberto, gesturing with his hand to punctuate his words. "Interest rates are low, and unemployment throughout Latin America continues to decline."

Unemployment may be declining, thinks Celeste, but not so the piece of elastic *morcilla* that her husband Roberto insists on chewing as he releases his words of wisdom. But he won't be the one eating the last bit on the plate, not because he doesn't like it, but because he is so engrossed in his parlance that he hasn't realized that there is a piece left. Who could imagine that this eloquent, daring lawyer is the most idealistic and absentminded man she has ever known? She often wonders how Roberto—whom she met while she was studying law in college—has gotten so far in his career, as he is so forgetful.

With her gaze still on the shriveled, black victim of human indifference, Celeste decides that no, Roberto would never eat that last piece. She feels pride in knowing that there aren't many men out there who would rather stand up for their ideas than eat tripe.

There is only one person left: Clara Ramos Pedraza. If there is someone at the table who couldn't care less about what people think, it's Clara, the feminist who had gotten a lot of press lately for defending domestic workers who file sexual harassment charges against their employers. It was Clara who had eaten the pork cracklings with no remorse, and licked each and every finger as if her life depended on it.

"The thing is, you only care about the economy," objects Clara her black, *morcilla*-encrusted teeth showing. "Since all you have are corporate clients…"

No one is fazed by Clara's remarks. Clearly, her sharp words no longer cut the way they used to. Celeste remembers the first time the group of co-working lawyers got together, some twenty years ago. They had agreed to meet each month after work for the purpose of bonding. In that very first get-together, Clara had not even finished her first drink when she called Carmen Rosín a disgrace to women exemplifying the role of submissive woman who flaunts her body to attain her goals. Carmen Rosín simply smiled, and from then on began wearing even more revealing outfits on the days when she did not have a court case.

"I bet Clara has been saying that all men are materialistic pigs and that women are mere objects," declares Carmen Rosín as she returns to the table, with no trace whatsoever of *morcilla* on her teeth.

Everyone remains silent, as if on cue. Acerbic remarks no longer put a damper on these gatherings. The trick is to ignore any insulting comments or simply order another round of drinks for the sake of the firm's harmony.

The waiter approaches the table demurely, with a demeanor learned in professional cooking schools. Celeste is intrigued by the way he then breaks all protocol and meticulously removes the men's plates from the table first. The waiter goes about in a systematic fashion, first seeking approval through eye contact with the seated male, then using his right hand—always to the left of the man—to remove the plate with great care. When he returns, he is more confident, and Celeste notices that the waiter takes seventy-three paces between the kitchen door and their table.

For the women, the waiter changes his rules of etiquette and doesn't even bother to look at them. He steps ups his pace as he removes the dishes, and takes merely fifty-one steps between the table and the kitchen. Why is that?, she wonders. Do cooking schools teach their students to hurry up when they remove a woman's dirty dishes?

The waiter appears one more time to take away the pink dish where the *morcilla* awaits its fate among congealed chunks of fat. Just as he is lifting the plate, a sharp and desperate "No!" stops him in his tracks. Someone grabs his hand firmly and he loses his balance. Inflation, unemployment, feminism—and even toothpicks—are put on hold.

Everyone at the table turns to find out what has happened.

With determination, Celeste stands up, grasping a fork in her hand. She smoothes her long, Boho skirt, leans over, and stabs the dark and furrowed victim. She shows off her prize to the others and, amid their astonished gazes, opens her mouth and does justice to the evening's martyr. And then, contented, Celeste gives her colleagues a *morcilla*-encrusted smile.

# PERFECTION

Still sweaty from labor, Rocío could not help but gaze into the eyes of the little bundle of joy she had just brought into this world. At that moment, she couldn´t have cared less whether her baby boy was missing a finger, or a toe, or even the family jewels of manhood between his legs.

With the doctor's consent, the nurse moved a little closer to carry the baby—whose name, the parents agreed, would be Ernestito—away to the nursery.

"Not just yet," said Rocío, reluctant to hand him over. "Experts agree that a baby shouldn't yawn during the first five minutes of his life. There are 90 seconds left to go."

Her husband, Ernesto, smiled; the doctor simply shrugged and left the room, not without patting the pediatrician on the back as a cue for him to examine the baby.

"He didn't yawn!" proclaimed Rocío after checking the time on her wristwatch.

Everyone clapped their hands, exchanging puzzled looks over the mother's concerns on yawning newborns. Five years ago, no one had looked at the clock after Claudia —Ernesto and Rocío's first child—was born.

They all sighed in relief once the pediatrician gave the baby a thumb's up. Rocío took the baby in her arms and smiled.

"So help me, I will never let you yawn," she swore solemnly.

Rocío's concern wasn't sheer whim. It came from an article she had read in a health magazine revealing a theory that European researchers had come up with after five decades of studying sonograms of fetuses in the womb. The doctors discovered that the fetuses that yawned the most in the womb would continue to yawn throughout their lives, and were less likely to succeed professionally. The study concluded, however, that if the parents were able to keep their baby from yawning during the first four years of his life, they would help ensure their child's success later on. The chances of success were better still if the baby did not yawn during the first five minutes after birth.

"I will never let my next child yawn," Rocío had sworn after reading the article.

Having lacked all this important information during her first pregnancy, Rocío insisted on opening a savings account for Claudia to pay for therapy and counseling in her adult years, in the event of a professional fiasco.

For Rocío's second pregnancy, things would be different. Not a day would go by without exposing her burgeoning belly to all types of music, art, children's books, and even literary classics such as *Don Quijote de la Mancha*. Her efforts paid off. None of the sonograms during Rocío's pregnancy showed even a hint of a yawn, much to the mother's delight.

Rocío went so far as to quit to her job as a chemist in order to stay at home and watch her child during the day. At night, a monitor and motion sensor in the baby's nursery helped her stay vigilant. At the slightest tremble of the baby's cheek, the signal of an upcoming yawn, Rocío would rush to the crib.

During his first three years and eleven months of life, Ernestito never, ever yawned. His mother made sure of that. She kept at least two of her child's senses busy at all times so that he wouldn't get bored. At the first sign of a sigh, as his mouth started to open, she would scramble to bring him his favorite plush toy or would switch on his beloved animal circus mobile that circled over his crib to the tune of Brahms' Piano Sonata in F Minor. Or, when running out of time, she would close his mouth firmly.

The day before Ernestito's fourth birthday, the father insisted that the two go out for the evening and leave the children with the nanny. Rocío agreed with him, thinking that there was little chance that Ernestito would yawn just hours before turning four. Besides, the last time the boy had even hinted at yawning was seven months ago.

With strict instructions from Rocío, the nanny agreed to stay a few extra hours with the children.

Mother and father were enjoying dinner with friends when they got a call from a distressed Claudia.

"What is it, dear?" asked Rocío, concerned.

"It's Ernestito," the child said. "He yawned!"

Rocío let out a cry and Ernesto shot up from his chair, ready to sprint to the car.

"What happened?" he asked.

"Ernestito yawned!" replied his troubled wife.

The couple flew out of the restaurant and got back home just in time to avert the catastrophe of another yawn. The nanny was sobbing. She assured the parents that she had followed their instructions and that as soon as the boy's cheek started to tremble, she had begun to sing, and clapped her hands to attract his attention. She even pulled out the old circus mobile from the trunk load of his baby things. She'd tried closing his mouth, but he bit her. The boy then opened his mouth in a wide yawn, and then another, and would laugh with each new yawn.

From that day on, Rocío never left his side. She lost count of the years, months and days since his fourth birthday. She opted for homeschooling when he yawned in preschool. But Ernestito yawned and kept on yawning, despite the subsequent line of tutors, educational trips to Europe, weekly visits to the theater, the opera, foreign film festivals, and art exhibits. She placed the boy in violin classes at the Music Conservatory. After his first yawn there, he was switched to the cello, then the flute, and then the piano, but he refused to practice and yawned through his lessons. He was placed in Tai Chi, oil painting, creative writing, soccer, and synchronized swimming classes, but to no avail. He showed no aptitude or interest. He yawned and kept on yawning.

Rocío became more and more distraught. She died of a massive heart attack following a particularly long, heart-felt yawn. Unable to cope with the loss, her husband died shortly after her.

Claudia had no need for the savings her parents had diligently been putting away for her throughout the years. She became an aerospace engineer after completing a doctorate in physics, and earned an international award for her research on the impact of gravity on the intensity and duration of a yawn.

Ernestito became her number one fan, while, between yawns, he continued to find his way through life.

# DUTY

It would have been an ordinary, uneventful Tuesday. The ashen clouds were soaking up the last remnants of a long winter. Wearing a dark blue dress and sneakers, Carolina was on her way to buy sushi to take back to the office, where her patients anxiously awaited their test results. She had the option of having someone bring her lunch, but she needed that thirty-minute break for stepping out of her daily routine and getting some fresh air and exercise. It was also her time to enjoy the privilege of anonymity in the Big Apple.

Carolina secured her smart phone's earbud so that Bon Jovi and the Rolling Stones could help her tune out the urban din. She walked two blocks to the small Korean deli, as she always did. The only change in habit that afternoon happened when she glanced to the left as she was passing by a music and video store. What caught her eye was the melancholic aspect of the elderly man seated inside the shop. His eyes compelled her to slow down the hurried pace that was helping her sail through the crowded sea of people, traffic lights and dazzling stores.

Judging by the man's collection of wrinkles and his slightly hunched-over posture, she estimated that he was about eighty. He was wearing a well-worn black corduroy suit and a black tie in an uneven red polka-dot print. He had lifted his gaze over the stack of CDs on the counter in front of him and was letting it wander outside the shop. Carolina keenly detected a black toupee. Next to the man, the cashier was reading the latest issue of *People* magazine. They were alone in that section of Latin American music.

There was something about that man's face, chiseled by dejection, that prompted Carolina to slow down. She tried to get on with her Tuesday routine, but that forlorn gaze stirred her emotions, in the same way a Pedro Flores song or a Gabriela Mistral poem often could. It was the same sensation she got finding that hidden box where she carefully guarded literary works by Cortázar, Benedetti, Neruda and Julia de Burgos, and the Polaroids that captured the special moments with her four siblings, such as the ones on rusty swings in the middle of an unkempt and puddled corner of a park in her Caribbean hometown.

Carolina pumped up the volume and kept walking. But fate—her fate—led her to turn back, and she found herself at the music shop's door. She went in. The man's gaze was still lost in the haste of the city. He didn't seem to be aware of what was going on inside the store, yet his outfit and his elegant style clearly begged for attention.

Carolina looked at him from the corner of her eyes, as she picked up a CD. She was convinced that she had seen him before, and searched her forty-something-year-old memory for answers. She knew that she would not find them in the last twenty years of her life, starred by her husband—a physician—, her nineteen-year-old daughter Kathy, her medical office on Fifth Avenue, the chalet in Colorado and her travels around the world. She paid no attention to the name of the singer on the CDs. She wanted to hunt for clues, slowly and deliberately.

Through the store's speakers, Carolina heard words that were once familiar - words marked by trilled "r's" and sharp syllables from a language she had repressed and replaced with another. It was one of the many measures she had taken in an attempt to bury her past.

*Gracias a tu mirada, tengo la esperanza de escapar este martirio. (Thanks to how you looked at me, I harbor hope of fleeing this martyrdom).*

Each word, each note took Carolina through a nostalgic journey. Recollections of her early childhood surfaced: the living room sofa upholstered in a flowery print, protected by plastic; mosquitoes; twisted palm fronds hanging from religious images on the wall; the floor with large tiles designed with black splotches that looked like worms. The center of attention was the record player next to the stacks of LPs. She remembered her father —dressed in a white, long-sleeved shirt and a black bowtie— leaving with his briefcase each day. Her mother would rush to the carport to make sure his Chevy was gone. Only then would she substitute the Daniel Santos or Maria Callas records for those of the singer with the robust and melodious voice. Her mother, shining with sweat, with her hair pinned up in a bun, would set down the cleaning cloth and furniture polish and sit on the rocking chair for a few seconds, closing her eyes and enjoying the music. In some instances, when she believed no one was looking, she would smoke while listening to that voice.

Carolina heard the loudspeaker announce that *La mirada*, on sale for $2.99, was now $1.99. It was then that it clicked. The singer of the CD on sale was he; the man in the black corduroy suit. The man whose music filled up her mother's afternoons.

As a child, she had always wondered why her mother hid that record filled with inciting and seductive songs. One day she searched until she found it. It was in the cabinet next to the record player, hidden between the lace tablecloths that had once belonged to her grandmother.

Carolina was only seven years old, but had carefully studied the man's face pictured on the record jacket, drawn to his perfect smile and the uncommon gleam in his eyes. He most certainly knew that countless women, like her mother, would desire him in secret, she thought. That was why he was smiling like that.

Carolina was unable to restrain her flowing memories. She recalled an afternoon on Pacífico del Norte Avenue. She and her older siblings were with their mother, waiting for the hoodless car carrying the singer on his first tour of the Caribbean. Thousands flocked to welcome *"El ídolo de América,"* America's idol, which was the moniker he was given through the magic of black-and-white television. Her mother, who until her death swore that he had looked at her when his car passed by, made her children promise that they would keep that pilgrimage a secret from their father. Carolina was not surprised by her mother's request because more than once, her drunken father had called *maricón,* the so-called *Ídolo de América*, even if he was married and had children. She remembered how her mother had kept her smile while hiding her fists behind her long skirt as he rattled on.

Another of his songs from the store's music system shook Carolina to the very core.

*Es ahora o nunca, te lo juro.*

*It's now or never, I swear to you,* she unconsciously translated.

Three years after the secret adventure at Pacífico del Norte Avenue, her mother started smoking in public and wearing mini-skirts; she would no longer hide the bruises under a longer skirt. She cut her hair and wore red lipstick. Carolina remembered the day, April 2, when her mother left the courthouse with her five children in tow, wearing a smile and no wedding ring. From that day on she no longer needed to hide the LPs.

Carolina looked at the singer and was overcome by a wave of grief and stifled sobs. The store was now full of tourists, college students and workers who were finding ways to do something different at lunchtime. She was certain that no one had noticed the jaded singer seated at a table in the Latin American section.

Holding back the tears, she took a deep breath and swallowed, to break the lump in her throat. With determination, she walked toward the table.

"My goodness, it's you!" she cried, opening her eyes and waving her arms to overstate her feigned excitement.

The singer turned to her slowly, as if life had stripped him of all sense of urgency. Slowly, his melancholy seemed to lift, and gave way to what Carolina thought was a hint of anticipation. The singer's face softened and even mustered the strength to smile.

Carolina's trembling hands scooped up four CDs from the table.

"I grew up listening to your songs," she told him in Spanish. "My mother was your number one fan."

The singer firmly clutched a pen, although his hands and his right leg were trembling. The cashier rushed in to help, but he gave her a frosty stare. She backed off timidly. The singer was finally able to remove the wrapping on one of the CDs and pull out the sleeve inside. He gave Carolina a questioning look.

"Uh, Carol Douglas," she said after a slight pause.

The singer gave her a quizzical look.

"Well, actually, my name is Carolina Pérez, but Caro will do," she said meekly. "Douglas is my husband's name."

Without erasing his smile, and feigning self-assurance, he autographed the CDs. Now, up closer, Carolina could see the scratches on his face from a clumsy shave. His perfect smile displayed a set of false teeth. Mouthwash had tried, in vain, to disguise the redolence of liquor, possibly vodka.

"My mother taught Spanish to elementary school children," Carolina continued in Spanish as she paid the cashier. "She took night courses to finish her studies."

The conversation in Spanish drew attention from the other clients in the shop. Some came closer to the table.

"If I hadn't come over I wouldn't have realized that it was you," said an elderly woman. "I saw you at Madison Square Garden thirty years ago."

"Oh, baby, it's you!" cried a sixty-something woman who came closer. "My wedding, your song *Locura*, you know, *la tocaron*. This is crazy. When I tell Papo I saw you *aquí*, wow!"

This time the singer smiled without effort. The store was playing another of his romantic songs: *Algo más te espera; sé valiente, te lo pido.* Carolina smiled to herself at the irony of the song's wording. *Something else awaits you; be brave, I beg you.*

"*Mira*. Look who's there! The real *Ídolo de América*," cried another woman. "I thought you were long gone."

"Those who call themselves *Ídolos de América* can't stand up to you," said a woman with a Colombian accent. "They're just mere clones."

Deciding it was time to go, Carolina wanted to look into the singer's eyes before leaving. She wasn't sure whether he had avoided looking at her. She took her bag and started heading toward the door. By then, the autograph line had grown longer. Before Carolina could leave, a woman tapped her shoulder.

"He wants to speak with you," she told Carolina, pointing toward the singer.

Puzzled, Carolina leaned closer. There was a CD on the table that the singer was pushing toward her with his finger, still avoiding her eyes. Carolina took it. It was titled *El deber. The duty.* She searched in her purse for money to pay, when she felt a firm but shaky hand that stopped her. Carolina looked into his eyes. Without needing an explanation, she left the store.

Outside, every step she took was a nostalgic sequence, one she had suppressed for so many years, beginning with innocence and followed by secrecy, terror, relief, happiness, uncertainty, release, and finally, freedom. She wanted to turn and see the singer's face one last time, but fear, her own, would not let her.

Shielded by the music from her cellphone, and just a block away from her office, Carolina sat down on the curb and opened the CD to see what the singer had written. The releasing power of so much repressed sorrow helped slowly unravel the knot in her throat. Not even at her mother's funeral eight years ago had she cried so much. She pulled off the earbuds, liberating her senses to reread the singer's words: *My dear Carolina Pérez, Thank you for making me feel again el Ídolo de América.*

*Forever yours.*

# FAME

After fourteen hours of labor, pushing to the encouraging choir of nurses, Catalina Román knew something was wrong when her husband uttered in a quavering voice: "You've just given birth to a beautiful girl, but what is that dreadful thing on your cheek?" There was no time to find out what Esteban was talking about.

It was undoubtedly a festive atmosphere. Newborn Rosa Clotilde was a beautiful baby, with fresh, rosy skin and big black eyes. She was so robust she looked like a five-month-old baby.

When all in the birthing room were done praising her beauty, Rosa Clotilde shocked them by turning on her side, raising her tiny hand and grabbing at the blooming warts on her mother's cheek. Catalina touched her cheek and felt two wrinkled, gravelly warts with dark, wiry hairs sprouting from the middle. She then understood her husband's words and let out a cry of horror that resonated throughout the birthing room and drowned out the Chopin sonata that, minutes before, had welcomed the baby. The nurses rushed to aid the mother, but chuckled after realizing that the new mother's main concern was her face.

"Catalina, this is normal after such a difficult labor," her doctor said. "Your warts should disappear in just a few days."

The new mother hoped that was true. She planned to resume her modeling career as soon as possible. She sighed with resignation and tried to show some warmth for the eight-pound bundle that had tugged on the heartstrings of everyone in the room.

Two months later, Catalina was visiting her dermatologist after a third wart, this one a bit fuzzier than the previous two, appeared on her face. In fact, it seemed as if the other two warts were thriving as well.

"It's just due to post-partum hormones," the dermatologist said. "Don't worry; they'll be gone soon."

After six months, the warts were still there and showed no signs of retreating. In fact, they were even enjoying the company of two new accomplices. Catalina stopped wearing facial cream, should that be the reason for her papules, but to no avail.

After seven months, much to her husband's relief, her concern shifted to her increasing weight. She had initially thought that baby-fat was still clinging to her body, but now she was sure that something was wrong after gaining forty-seven pounds in such short time.

The editor of True Vanities, a magazine that Catalina had once posed for, called to invite her to pose with Rosa Clotilde for the Mother's Day edition. With resignation over the double whammy of warts *and* weight, Catalina agreed to do the shoot, but warned that she was still recovering from childbirth. On the day of the photo session, she posed with huge sunglasses that partially covered the tubers on her right cheek. She hid her ample figure under a gypsy tunic that Esteban had given her. She believed the shoot went well, but her delight turned to disappointment when the published edition featured only Rosa Clotilde on the cover, as if she had no mother and had been brought into this world by a stork. It was the first time that the magazine's Mother's Day edition published a lone baby on the cover, and sold out quickly. Rosa Clotilde became so popular that she was hired by a baby-food company for a new ad campaign. She behaved so well, so perfectly, so lovingly during the shoot that the entire production crew was enchanted and gave her a gigantic teddy bear.

Encouraged by her baby's popularity, Catalina upped her efforts at losing the additional fifty-seven pounds she had now gained that jiggled conspicuously all over her. She spent three hours a day with a personal trainer at the gym, huffing and puffing to the rhythm of her favorite tunes. She instructed her cook to prepare only vegetarian dishes devoid of all fat and sugar.

In a month, her husband Esteban had lost eighteen pounds; Catalina, meanwhile, had put on that very same amount of weight. Esteban suspected that his wife was snacking behind his back, so he hired a private eye who not only watched her every move, but also installed hidden cameras in every corner of the house. A month later, the solemn PI could only state that the wife was definitely not noshing on forbidden foods in the dark.

"It's a curse," she cried. "As much as I try to lose weight, I'm only getting fatter."

In fact, a year since the baby was born, Catalina had put on ninety-seven pounds, at least three of which belonged to the nine warts that were now colonizing her cheek. Even Esteban was convinced that the baby had hexed her mother: for every pound that Rosa Clotilde gained, Catalina put on another six. The pediatrician couldn't understand why the young mother would break into tears every time he weighed the baby.

But in time, Catalina began to accept her condition and her new body. She acquired a taste for wide tunics and even mustered the courage to choose one in a deep purple shade, daring enough to display her curves and her prominent cleavage. She mastered the art of wearing wide-brimmed hats to draw attention away from her warts. And when she could not hide them she flaunted them by dabbing bright colors on them, making them appear as if they were stray moons in a newborn galaxy.

She started to enjoy going out again, and even got used to the astonished looks on people's faces when they saw her dramatic appearance. It pleased her to see that people's eyes were not merely focusing on Rosa Clotilde anymore but were also spontaneously resting on her ample curves and her sculpted visage.

"You have guts to go out that way," said her friend Emilia Casiano one evening. "I wouldn't have the courage."

"I've had no choice," Catalina replied. "If Heaven is testing me by giving me such a beautiful baby, and changing my body and face this way, then so be it!"

Soon, Rosa Clotilde learned to count to fourteen using her mother's warts like the beads of an abacus. Catalina, meanwhile, began to truly enjoy being with her baby and forgot her conviction that she had been hexed. Her husband became her number one fan, celebrating each new wart with a bouquet of daisies, her favorite flower.

One winter day, Catalina awoke with a renewed desire to sing. She had agreed to be interviewed by Federico Neico, one of TV's most prominent reporters, host of the top-rated One on One show. It would be twenty minutes dedicated only to her; she was not told to bring her baby. For the occasion, she decided to wear her most colorful tunic, in a bright green-and-red print with blue stripes and yellow and black polka dots. She took extra care putting on her makeup, making sure to highlight each and every one of her furry facial tubers.

Hundreds of fans were already waiting for her at the TV station when she arrived. Amid the crowd she saw a sign that read: "We are with you, Catalina." Many of the women were wearing tunics in vivid colors and makeup that highlighted their warts and moles. Blowing kisses from a distance, Catalina swung her hips as she walked to the studio door. Even the station's highest executives took a break from their busy schedules to shake Catalina's hand and take selfies with her. Federico Neico escorted Catalina to Studio B, where the cheers and ovations from the audience brought tears to her eyes that formed small puddles between her warts. The director wasted no time in starting the production.

"It is our pleasure to have you on our show," said Neico.

"Oh, the pleasure is mine," she replied.

"Now, tell us a bit about yourself. What happened to the former Catalina, the one with perfect measurements and the lovely face?"

"It's a long story. My body changed after I gave birth."

"But those extra pounds and those warts are your new signature," said Neico. "I understand that you have fans who have undergone surgery to add warts to their faces."

She would never forget how, at that precise moment, she felt a slight tingling on her face. Discreetly, she touched her cheek, wondering if a mosquito was biting one of her warts.

"And what does your husband have to say about your look?"

"He still loves me. He says that whatever makes me happy makes him happy."

Catalina felt another tingle, slightly above the first spot. But what alarmed her was the sudden jolt on her left buttock. It was impossible that she had been kicked accidentally in that area; there was no one close enough.

"Have doctors been able to determine the reasons for all these changes?" asked Neico.

"Oh, they have run the battery of tests. All show nothing and..."

Catalina's felt her left side suddenly deflate. Surprised, Neico jumped from his chair and grabbed her by the arm. As he tried to keep his balance, he apologized and ordered a commercial break.

"Are you okay, Catalina? Would you like some water?"

"I feel funny," she said.

"Nerves can get the best of us, so just relax. Everything will be just fine."

Catalina looked with confusion at the show host.

"I guess it's my nerves. Something strange is happening to me."

"Don't worry. We are just about to wrap it up."

Once back on air, Catalina concentrated on the interview in order to forget the untimely jolts and deflations that were tormenting her. But she couldn´t help letting out a moan when she felt a hot tingle on her densely-populated cheek. Thinking that her nerves were acting up again, Neico gave her a reassuring smile and a wink.

"Catalina, how does it feel to be a different kind of woman?"

"Oh, it feels great. At first, I didn't like it, but then I got used to it…

"Oh!"

"What happened?" Neico asked alarmed.

"Excuse me," she whispered. "I feel a terrible itch on my cheek. If I scratch it I'll ruin my makeup."

"Folks, we'll be back after this break."

Stunned, Neico was the first to notice Catalina's transformation. She had instantly shed dozens of pounds, and her clothes were now hanging from her body. Layers of makeup were sliding off her face. And then her warts began popping, one after another, giving off a bluish green ooze that was staining her voluminous dress.

"What is happening to you? Jesus, Catalina, what's going on?" yelled Esteban rushing to his wife.

Catalina felt strange sensations throughout her body, but she was not able to fully understand what was going on. She let out an enormous cry, though, when a staff member gave her a mirror.

"Catalina, this is a disaster. You've ruined our show!" Neico said.

The show's producer snapped out of her daze and ordered the staff to continue airing Catalina's transformation. Viewers across the country witnessed the moment when Catalina, amid sobs and tears, realized what was happening to her.

"Good God! What have you done to me? Where have my warts and my rolls of fat gone? What will become of my fame?"

The producer slapped Neico out of his stupor, pointing urgently at Catalina.

"It's a miracle, ladies and gentlemen!" cried Neico. "Catalina has gotten her figure and face back. And no warts!"

The camera took a close up of Catalina so that audiences could see the expression of horror on her face, her melting makeup, and her unblemished skin.

"You have recovered your beauty!" her husband cried. "It's my Catalina again!"

The station's receptionist rushed onto the set yelling that thousands of viewers had threatened to storm the premises, demanding the "real" Catalina again. Heartbroken, Catalina sank into the yards of fabric she had once filled that were now flowing around her. Before passing out, she swore that she would some day be beautiful again.

# ESSENCE

Marta's attention was drawn back to the game show splashed across her digital TV screen. The show's host was instructing the two women finalists to stuff their unrefined but no less willing mouths with Golden Age barbecue-flavored potato chips. The winner would be the first gorged mouth able to enunciate the phrase "Sensational Saturday is a spectacularly super show," sputtering as few crumbs as possible.

Dressed to kill in a blue jumpsuit, the chubby lady became the easy winner of a four-inch radio that featured a built-in digital clock. The otherwise lively audience was stunned. It seemed that there was something to those rosy cheeks after all, because the woman delivered the tongue twister fluently, without spitting so much as four ounces of zero trans-fat mush. Her competitor, a young pregnant woman who only managed to mumble that her name was Carmencita, spewed the mashed contents of her mouth onto the small tray placed under her chin, and caused an uproar on the set when that very same mouth, in a contorted grimace, then threatened to deposit her lunch right in front of the cameras. The production crew broke into frenzy, fearing the worst as visions of the station's cafeteria menu —mondongo tripe, pig's feet with chickpeas, pigeon peas, and even pork sausage—flashed before their very eyes.

Amid sobs, the trembling Carmencita pleaded for one last chance. After giving her a pat on the back so that she could release the words "I beg you," Noel, the young show host, shook his head. A unanimous gasp was heard from the audience, but the producer sighed in relief. It was a well-known secret that any display of pity on a television set was to last no more than a few seconds, for the sake of ratings.

And so, the young woman left with the complete satisfaction of knowing that her consolation prize—a basket full of 16-ounce cans of soup—was an acknowledgement of her gargantuan effort on TV. It really didn't matter to Carmencita that her basket had one less can of soup than that of last week's runner-up, because she would spend the rest of her days telling everyone she knew how the audience had given her a well-deserved ovation.

"At last, this torture is over," Marta thought to herself. The evening news was coming up, which would include a small segment from her latest conference on the literature of the Spanish Golden Age. On the other side of the room her husband, Miguel, was immersed in a crossword puzzle. She was only able to see his right foot, propped on a cushion next to the red roses. Beethoven's Symphony no. 9 in D Minor was wafting from the stereo.

"Man of La Mancha," he mumbled. "Don Quixote."

A commercial touting cold beer made Marta realize how thirsty she was. She stood up and immediately felt a jolt. The honorable and restrained Noel was on the screen, pointing at her.

"Ma'am, it's your turn now. Luisa, bring the barbecue-flavored potato chips for our next contestant."

Marta could not believe that Carmencita's mumbling lines had not put an end to the mortifying torture. Wasn't one humiliation a day enough?

"Ma'am, please step forward. We are waiting for you." It seemed as if the emcee were speaking directly to her. Marta scoffed at such a thought, and imagined how ridiculous she'd look on that set.

"Marta de Vega, we are waiting for you," said Noel.

Marta de Vega? Just like her, huh? Apparently, it was a common name. So there goes what her parents thought was an original name.

"What are you waiting for, ma'am? C'mon down. This is your chance to win a GE toaster, complete with a built-in fire alarm."

"Who in their right mind would even consider adding a fire alarm to a toaster?" wondered Marta, just as she was getting up from the sofa to fetch a cold bottle of Japanese beer.

It so happened that her left foot was the first part of her body to go through the screen. Screaming, Marta grabbed the arm of the sofa, but felt the urgency of the rest of her body to follow the wandering foot. She called out to her husband, but her voice got lost in the audience's screams. Her left hand followed, even though Marta resisted. In a matter of seconds, Marta found herself on the set, welcomed by a warm ovation, a bag of potato chips, and the audience's enthusiastic cries of "Barbecue chips!"

"Marta, you are tonight's lucky contestant. You could win a toaster with a built-in fire alarm. Is your family here with you?" asked Noel.

Still in shock trying to figure out what was happening, Marta scanned the audience and couldn't find any familiar faces. She blinked several times to see if the act will wake her up from the nightmare.

"No," she answered after realizing the blinking did not deliver the desired result.

"Would you like to say hello to them?"

Slowly coming out of her stupefaction, Marta realized the television set and the barbecue chips had become her immediate reality. This was also her long-awaited chance to show the audience and the other contestants the art of articulating complex and clever sentences. But instead, annoyingly, she found herself repeating the usual contestants greeting: "I'd like to say hello to my family."

"Very well, Marta. You have forty seconds to stuff your cheeks with barbecue-flavored potato chips and say: 'Sensational Saturday is a spectacularly super show.' Our assistant, Luisa, will place a tray under your chin. And we'll see just how much mush you can hold in when you say the phrase. If you spit out fewer crumbs than our first contestant, you will win the toaster."

Marta pinched herself, wondering whether she was dreaming. She wasn't. She looked at the 64-ounce bag of chips and wondered why in the world did they have to be barbecue flavored. Why couldn't she have the option of choosing sour cream or cheese? Or maybe *manchego* cheese, as it goes so well with a glass of merlot.

Encouraged by the audience's sincere applause, Marta was about to begin stuffing her mouth.

"Remember, Marta, do not swallow the potato chips. We know that Golden Age potato chips are everybody's favorite, but the goal here is not to see whether you like them, but rather to find out how much room you have in those cheeks of yours."

Marta soon realized that putting all those chips into a single mouth required a lot of effort. Nevertheless, she savored how good they really tasted. Would they have an organic version? she wondered as she tried not to swallow all that crunchy saltiness and attempted, instead, to push every last one into all the nooks and crannies of her pie hole.

The first batch was easy to accommodate behind her left wisdom tooth. She pushed the second handful behind her right wisdom tooth. Her biggest challenge, however, was to make sure that the pasty portion patted against her top teeth stayed put.

"Ten seconds left, Marta."

The audience joined in the countdown and shouted out the unmerciful numbers: "...seven, six, five, four...!"

She had only a few seconds left to force the bag's remaining crumbs into her mouth and push them under her tongue. It was just in the nick of time because together, the host and the audience cried: "Zero!"

Marta glanced at her image on one of the monitors. She congratulated herself for still wearing the string of pearls and the beige outfit that she had on for her conference earlier that day. Her golden hair and red lipstick now highlighted her heavy, flushed jowls.

"Well, well. Marta was able to fill her cheeks with the whole bag of the best potato chips in the world: Golden Age potato chips, barbecue flavored. Now comes the hard part. Luisa, please bring the tray."

A drumroll beckoned the audience to join in a cheer that echoed throughout the open-air stadium where at least thirty thousand people had gathered to witness the event. "Marta! Marta! Marta!" they clamored.

Her success now depended on how deeply she could concentrate. She remembered her Yogi's teachings, which came in handy for less mystical endeavors such as this.

Marta was trying to master the art of masticating mush and did not think twice before placing her chin on the cold tray.

Its coldness yanked her out of her concentration for a second, but Marta quickly recalled her Yogi's lesson of mind over body, and at once returned to her mashed-up reality, which consisted of an impressive amount of chewed chips plastered on her teeth and mouth roof. She could not decide which effort was greater: resisting her gustatory desire to push the pasty meal down her esophagus and thus continue the digestive process, or to resume the colossal effort to maintain her concentration.

*Concentrate.* Marta closed her eyes, silently repeating her mantra: *Om saha nāvavatu, Saha nau bhunaktu.*

She felt a zap of energy. Marta imagined that she was climbing a steep mountain and after reaching the deserted top, she contemplated the vastness, feeling as if she were literally on top of the world.

The compact mass in the back of her mouth started making room for the one in the front, thus freeing her tongue for the awaited finale. Marta awoke from her vision. In her usual clear and perfect diction, she responded to the euphoric clamor of the audience, pronouncing: "Sensational Saturday is a spectacularly super show."

The camera first took a shot of her mouth, then her encrusted teeth. And then it focused on the empty tray. A hush overtook the audience when they realized that there was not even a crumb on the tray.

"Marta, you are the proud winner of a GE toaster, complete with a fire alarm!" Noel finally managed to say after staring in disbelief at the empty tray. "Congratulations!"

Marta observed the immaculate tray and flashed a barbecue-flavored smile. As if on cue, the audience rushed to greet her. Without lifting their astonished gaze from the tray, the security guards formed a tight circle around Marta. Noel asked the audience to calm down, promising each person a 16-ounce bag of Golden Age potato chips. He had to supersize his offer to 32-ounce bags to pacify the public.

"Again, Marta, congratulations! In the thirteen years this show has been on the air, you are the first contestant to keep absolutely everything in her mouth. Would you like to say a few words?"

Gesturing with her hand, Marta asked for some time-out. In her usual ladylike demeanor, she delicately swallowed the last vestiges of mush, and, turning her face from the cameras, she used her pinkie nail to pick out the more obvious crumbs from her teeth. With the aplomb of someone accustomed to wagging her tongue inside unusually inflated cheeks, Marta de Vega now faced the cameras and grabbed the microphone.

"I wish to thank my family for their full support in all my important endeavors," she said emotionally as the magnitude of her most recent achievement started to sink in.

She could now see among the audience the faces of Miguel and their two sons, Luis Miguel and Miguel Luis, beaming with pride. She started to run toward them, but stopped in her tracks when she saw the bikini-clad Luisa arriving with the toaster, complete with a fire alarm. Her eyes now welling with tears, Marta carefully cradled the toaster, kissed it, and held it over her head in a sign of victory. Seeing how her act of reverence moved the enthusiastic audience, the ecstatic Marta fell to her knees, and the toaster's fire alarm went off.

# HABIT

Despite her best efforts, Elena Rubí was only able to make out shadows through the iron grates. Sometimes they resembled waves flowing onto shore, as if life were continuing its course, she thought to herself. Haven't they realized that the Earth doesn't spin as it used to, and that believing otherwise and clinging to an old habit is simply insane? Was she the only one anticipating the looming catastrophe that was about to happen?

Elena Rubí sat down again on the hard cot that took up half of her cell. She had been locked up simply for demanding her rights as an individual. But she felt some comfort. At least she was assigned to a cell with a toilet and a shower, and she was allowed to keep her black, tailored dress. But, as with any other inmate, the jail wardens meticulously inspected every inch of her clothes.

She wanted to know what time it was to determine how much longer she had to wait for her lawyer. Each new inmate was allowed a phone call, and she was granted that right, in spite of the national emergency. She figured she would not have to testify to the injustice that had sparked the crisis because Earth had little time left, that is, if everyone insisted on clinging to insanity.

Elena Rubí made her cot with a faded sheet, the only one she was given. She folded her linen blazer like a pillow and lay down. It was now time to forget the irrational behavior of authorities, and ponder the day's events.

The reason for her imprisonment was easy to identify. The previous morning had begun as usual for a Wednesday in February of a leap year, with the customary rainfall. The pitter-patter of the raindrops on the terrace's tin roof made Elena Rubí cozy up in her sheets to enjoy the morning rain. Later, after four hours of imprisonment, she would figure out that there had been something different that morning that had changed her routine. Something about that particular rainfall; the pause between each drop had lasted three seconds when it normally lasted two. She knew that well, after years of keeping track of the time between raindrops as a way to lull her self back to sleep. She had thought that the change in pattern was due to the wind rocking the old roof. She now knew better.

Elena Rubí remembered that the first thing she did when she got up yesterday morning was to look at the clock sitting next to the book she was reading that week: *Eight Rules for the Efficient Woman*. Instead of waking her three children, Dolores, José and Humberto, with the usual wake-up call, she sang them a lullaby and deposited three-and-a-half kisses on each one's cheek. Looking in the bathroom mirror, she noticed that there was something different. The mirror, perhaps? Her face? No. It was a regular day. She grabbed her toothbrush and emptied a small dollop of hand soap on it. She brushed her teeth, then gargled with dandruff shampoo. She squeezed a generous amount of toothpaste on to her hands and plastered her face with it. It was enough to banish the dark circles under her eyes and lift any oil and dirt from her face. From the bathroom, Elena Rubí beamed with pride at the sound of her three children getting ready for school.

That morning, she'd left her bedroom dressed in a pink lamé gown. She walked to the large kitchen with the dark granite countertops that her husband had bought for their fifteenth wedding anniversary. She removed a steak from the refrigerator and placed it over the stove flame. She then set the table before the kids came down from their rooms and rushed to the laundry room, where she fed the dryer with dirty laundry and baptized the heap of clothing with a generous cup of pet flea shampoo. The children realized something was wrong, not because their mother was dressed in an elegant gown or because she was reeking of toothpaste, but because of the way she prepared breakfast.

"Mom!" cried Dolores. "What *is* this?"

Elena Rubí heard the urgent tone in her youngest daughter's voice and laughter from her other children. She rushed into the kitchen. She looked at the table, but nothing really stood out.

"Is it too hot?"

Dolores looked at her mother in that particular way a child of eight does at six in the morning.

"Where's my cereal?"

"What's wrong with the steak?" replied Elena Rubí puzzled.

"That's not breakfast."

Elena Rubí made an effort to understand her daughter's words, but she could not see what the problem was.

"Says who? Where is it written that you must have cereal for breakfast?" she replied. Her children were baffled and concerned, but they also seemed to be enjoying themselves.

José got up and went to the laundry room.

"Mom, what's going on?" he cried.

Elena Rubí found her children's unusual behavior confusing.

She rushed over to find José in front of the dryer, gingerly picking up his black pants with his finger and thumb. The pants had two very prominent mud stains on the knees and were dripping wet with some kind of liquid.

"What's the problem?"

"My pants aren't clean. They're full of mud and a strange wet stuff," he replied, confused.

The three children looked at their mother in astonishment. Dolores opened the washer and gasped when she saw that it was filled with packages of cheese and raw meat. Elena Rubí looked at her children for a brief instant, then turned and faced the industrial-sized washer and dryer.

"Everything's fine. They're working perfectly," she said, relieved.

The kids decided that their mother was just playing a few pranks and got ready for school. Humberto didn't even bat an eye when his mother put a shirt in the blender instead of ironing it. No one said a word when Elena Rubí packed their lunch bags with high-calcium dog biscuits and birdseed. They sighed in relief when she ordered them all to get into the car, just like any other day.

But the fun and games came to a halt when Elena Rubí pulled up in front of the park where they practiced sports in the evenings, instead of at school. Being the older brother, Humberto looked at his siblings and signaled for them to get out of the car. Once Elena Rubí drove off, Humberto called his father and told him what had just happened.

Back home, Elena Rubí was still trying to understand why her kids had acted the way they did. What difference did it make if they practiced sports in the morning and went to school in the afternoon? What was the problem with wearing their school uniforms for baseball practice? Where was it written that this could not be the order of things?

An hour later, on her way to the office, Elena Rubí paid no attention to her ringing cell phone. She didn't even wince when her co-workers gawked at her for coming to work in a long, flowing cotton gown from India over her one-piece bathing suit. She even had sunglasses, a wide-brimmed sun hat and a bottle of cold Chablis under her arm.

The words *Assistant Director* were emblazoned on her office door. She went in, took off her gown and sat in her chair, turning it toward the window to soak up the sun that was just beginning to filter through the immaculately clean glass.

Neither the secretary nor the second assistant director were able to convince her that the 23rd floor of Government Iron Tower I was no place for sunbathing.

"Where is it written that you can't sunbathe here?" said Elena Rubí, while slathering on plenty of sunscreen. The secretary came in with a distraught look on her face to tell her that she had an urgent call from her husband. Elena Rubí was unfazed.

"Tell him that he knows I don't answer any calls while I'm sunbathing."

With each passing minute, the employees grew more concerned over the sudden change in the woman who, until that day, had been an excellent civil servant in the state's insurance regulations agency. They could hear blaring salsa music coming from Elena Rubí's office. The strong staccato of her heels was an unequivocal sign that she was dancing to her heart's content.

Her husband, Pedro Jesús, arrived at the office around ten, a welcome relief for the employees. He searched their faces for an explanation.

"She's lost it," said the secretary.

"What is going on?" he asked. "The kids said that she was behaving strangely this morning. She left them at the park instead of at school."

Raúl Manuel, the agency's director, arrived at that very minute, accompanied by a security guard.

"What is going on?" asked the guard.

"She was fine when I left the house this morning," said Elena Rubí's husband curtly. "I'll go in first."

"Would you like the guard to go in with you?" asked Raúl Manuel.

"For God's sake, of course not! She's probably pulling our leg."

Pedro Jesús went into the office with the authority of a husband and the vice president of a company. He was struck by the blaring sound of salsa and the scent of incense. His wife was dancing in her bathing suit on five-inch high heels.

"Elena! Elena Rubí!"

It was not until he had cried out Elena Rubí for the third time that she stopped wiggling. She looked at him.

"What are you doing here?"

Suffice it to say, there was no way to make her understand it was she who was engaging in unacceptable behavior, and not her co-workers, as she argued. Elena Rubí pulled out her contract from the file cabinet and very eloquently argued that nowhere throughout the fifty-four clauses did it say that she couldn't get a tan, play music, or dance in her office. Pedro Jesús shrugged and called work to say that he would be out for the rest of the day; he needed to solve a personal matter.

"She's your employee, so deal with it," he told the security guard before rushing out to go pick up the kids.

An hour later, Elena Rubí left work without saying goodbye. Everyone in the office sighed with relief. They could now go back to typing, and to escaping to the cafeteria under the blessing of their labor union contracts.

Unaware of the problems she was causing, Elena Rubí tried to deposit a check at the Number 3 checkout aisle in her favorite supermarket. Later, after standing in line for twenty-three minutes, she was escorted out of a bank because the teller was unable to convince her that they did not sell milk or *serrano* ham there.

It was on the 10-o'clock news that her co-workers, friends, and family found out about what the anchorman called "the telenovela of the woman named Elena Rubí."

"Thousands of people, dressed in cartoon-character pajamas, gathered outside the metropolitan women's detention center demanding the release of Elena Rubí Delgado. For the second time today, the governor activated the National Guard. This measure was taken hours after a riot broke out earlier this afternoon near the Capitol Building, when Elena Rubí Delgado, a young mother of three from San Juan with no criminal record, insisted on obtaining a vehicle permit for her Hello Kitty bag at the Senate chairman's office. She argued that there is no law prohibiting her from buying it there and pasting the permit on her bag. Because of her high-ranking government position, the thirty-seven-year-old woman was able to reach the chairman's office without arousing suspicion, despite the fact that she was wearing yellow Sponge Bob pajamas and Barney slippers. Three employees tried unsuccessfully to explain that vehicle permits were not sold in that office. The woman insisted that there was nothing about that in the Constitution, and repeatedly cited: 'The will of the people is the source of public power; the political order is subordinate to the rights of man, and the free participation of citizens in collective decisions is assured.' The Police Riot Squad was summoned to the scene when hundreds of people stormed the

Capitol demanding vehicle permits after they were informed about Elena Rubí's case through the social media. The woman left the building only after finally getting a permit and pasting it on her Hello Kitty bag. The suspect was taken to the women's detention center after being involved in another incident this evening, when she arrived at the Ernesto de la Vara school to pick up her children. She was wearing a black, tailored suit and had brought a pot of fresh oatmeal. She began to strike the windows after finding out that the school was closed. The suspect insisted that it was time to release her children. She was arrested for disturbing the peace and climbed into the police car shouting that everyone was crazy, that the world was coming to an end, and asking where were all those rules written."

*\*\**

Elena Rubí sighed in relief when the prison guard and the social worker opened her cell door.

"The psychiatrist testified that you are saner than many other people out there," said the social worker. "You are free to go."

Elena Rubí felt much calmer and put her hands together to pray. Solemnly, she knelt before the toilet.

"Thank you, Santa Claus, for enlightening them and making them understand not all is written," she said.

# THE ENCOUNTER

That certain tingle ventures into even the most secretive corner of my whole being; a tingle that I wish would go on forever.

Your hand timidly glides up my left thigh and yearns to know whether there is red-blooded life flowing through these veins of mine. I fidget: a sign that passion is rising from underneath my skin, elicited by the thrill of feeling something new, something exciting.

Your hand abruptly stops mere inches from my red-light district. There are no neon lights beckoning you to continue your daring search. I wonder whether you will continue or back off. I mean, if you were bold enough to let your turquoise-blue blanket fall casually on my lap so that you could slide your hand up my thigh, I can't see any reason for you to stop now.

I decide to pretend that I am still napping and my own reaction surprises me. Only seconds earlier I had thought that the exotic but familiar energy growing between my legs was merely a dream. All I have to do is to open my eyes for a few seconds to realize that my exotic world is just a passenger bus taking me through a continent that three weeks ago I was unfamiliar with. To my right, the Andes greet me, and at my back, the Chilean city of Temuco is still bidding me a long farewell.

My sense of propriety tries to tackle my passion and my first thought is to shoot back a few words in your direction and alert the driver of your brazen behavior. But I can't decide what to do, not out of fear, but because I like what I feel and I am intrigued to find out how far you will go.

I close my eyes again, and while your hand is still provoking me, I try to remember your face, the one I glanced at for a few seconds before you boarded the bus. I saw how you placed your old, leather backpack and guitar in the cargo trunk after patiently waiting for a small, elderly woman to find room for her suitcase, with some help. The woman's mixed ethnicity and her poised demeanor called my attention, but I was not able to pull out my camera in time to capture her expression and render it into a piece of art.

You helped her board the bus when you saw that I was watching. I tried to hide the camera, but the woman saw me and refused to sit next to me. You sat next to me instead, settling in with a thick book in your hands. Soon enough, the musky smell of your coat hit my nostrils. These three weeks of travel have taught me to accept that smell as peculiar to winter in this part of the world. Your hair is long, that I remember. I would give anything to study your features and your face; but then I would lose that magic, that anonymous exchange that you and I now have.

My body has not moved an inch since it felt your hand. I'm afraid the magic will be over if I squirm more than I have to. My career and my upbringing helped with my composure. Your hand is now warm but lifeless on my red-light district. I must admit that I don't care. I sense by the rhythmic movement of your seat that your other hand is happily resting between your legs, secluded under your blue blanket.

I'm dying to know whether the slight moan I hear comes from you, so close yet so distant.

Do you feel the same way I do, even though my hand does not respond in the same fashion?

I hear voices that come closer. You remove your hand nonchalantly and let the blanket fall casually to the floor. Although I still pretend to be asleep, I'm now glad; the blanket was becoming nuisance. The bus stops and the inside lights take turns going on from the back of the bus to the front, like the first lighting up of a Christmas tree. I decide to stay completely still to savor the gush of pleasure.

You get up without turning toward me, and stretch leisurely. You leave the bus, calmly, as if you were just waking from a long and sweet nap. I realize that I will not get to know the protagonist of this unusual, exciting episode. You don't even turn to take one last look at the latest object of your shameless desire.

I discreetly fix my skirt and settle in my seat for a few more hours of travel. The harder I try to doze off, the more convinced I am that the insolent encounter between your hand and my body was simply meant to be.

# LIBERATION

Having arranged her abundant tresses, Carmen Luisa sits down again in front of her computer screen, a feat she can easily accomplish despite the confined dimensions of her tiny office. She puffs out her chest with pride as she gazes at the dozens of trophies and awards she has received both locally and abroad as a journalist. Behind her desk are rows of shelves containing works of literature and a collection of detective novels, which are barely visible behind the myriad photos of her beloved children and grandchildren.

Carmen Luisa looks at the clock. Only forty-three minutes left before her deadline. She sighs and reads through the article she has written, down to the very last line: "The governor stated that the economy will finally shake free of its recession by next year's final quarter."

She pauses, looks at her right hand, and once again counts her fingers. It's a habit of hers. She laughs inwardly at the thought of someone discovering her bizarre ritual, which involves only her right hand. Thanks to human symmetry, she has no reason to count the fingers of her left hand. All five fingers of her right hand, crowned by neatly groomed nails painted a delicate pink, are still there. They may be fragile, but they are loyal. Her ring finger displays a simple wedding band.

Carmen Luisa looks at her story. She feels a sudden jolt, and mumbles to herself, realizing that it's only her left hand, which her doctor says is beginning to show early signs of rheumatoid arthritis. As a matter of fact, her doctor mentioned that it was the first time in his career that he had seen a case involving only one hand.

Her left hand, which moments ago was resting on her thigh to alleviate numbness, is now tapping away at the keyboard, as if possessed by a high-spirited demon. Confused, Carmen Luisa looks at the screen and sees new sentences emerging beneath her article:

Paola María was donning her pajamas when she heard a blunt thud which she thought had come from her study.

Carmen Luisa's jaw drops almost to the ground. She looks carefully at her left hand. Its fingers are now thick and twisted, with three-inch long vibrant red acrylic nails adorned with tiny gold and silver stars. The pinky lags behind because it is hauling a faux multi-carat diamond rock, while the index finger sports barbed wire for a make-believe ring. The ring finger, meanwhile, looks as if it is on the verge of a breakdown, as it attempts to skirt the wire.

Carmen Luisa feels a rush of panic. She looks carefully at her surroundings. Yes, she is still in her office, and no, time has not stopped, as she is able to follow her wall clock's second hand for a whole minute. She closes and opens her eyes, but the emerging text and her disfigured southpaw are still there, indifferent to her angst. Is she hallucinating? Is this a symptom of her early rheumatoid arthritis? Did she take the wrong dose of medication for her condition?

She returns to the keyboard, attempting to include an economist's viewpoint on the economy: "Regardless of the government's austerity measures and its public investment plans, the recession will only worsen throughout the following months, thus leading to a rise in unemployment."

But her left hand rises in protest and goes back to typing. Carmen Luisa abruptly slaps it aside and encourages her always clever right hand to continue writing. An evil spirit again takes charge of her left, which not only strikes her right hand, but also scratches it with the fury of decades of pent-up loathing. The right hand gives up in pain; its bored index finger delicately licks the more noticeable cuts. Drops of blood fall on the keyboard while the left hand starts typing.

Carmen Luisa looks at the screen and is surprised to see the writing:

> The thud had come from the adjacent room, which Paola María, a rookie journalist, found odd because there was nobody there.
> The room's only occupants were a desk, a chair, and several gray filing cabinets, each with three drawers...

Shaken, Carmen Luisa jumps up from the chair. She tries to pull her left hand away from the keyboard, but it will not budge. In fact, it holds on to the keyboard and loses two of its magnificent nails, unfortunately. In a futile attempt at demanding order and respect, the right hand tries to grab its twisted twin, but the left fights back. Fearing it will lose one of its blushing nails, the right hand retreats and settles near its mistress's hip. The battle has ended, and Carmen Luisa has no other choice but to sit down, hoping that it was a hallucination and that it will soon end. But when she looks at the screen she is horrified by what her left hand has written:

Paola María entered the room and found the body of the Mexican journalist Amanda Reguero Fortuna near the desk. She knew right then and there that it was Amanda, because she was wearing her usual gold-rimmed sunglasses. Paola María was shaken.

She blinked to make sure that the two glasses of merlot reserve were not playing tricks on her. Why was this body, complete with sunglasses, in the study of her home? Her first thought was to call the police, and to keep the integrity of what looked like a crime scene. As she went to pick up the phone, she noticed that the computer was on. As she came closer, she realized that the screen was flashing words in Times New Roman 72: "Traitor. Don't betray your true calling."

Paola María's left brain, the one with the common sense, signaled her to stay away. But the utter curiosity of her right brain won the upper hand. Paola María buttoned her pajama shirt to the top, then crossed herself. She wrapped her right index finger in a towel and gently tapped the cursor to find out what else was written at the top of the document. She read the first few lines: "Violence from the Sicilian mafia is sweeping onto our shores, with at least three murders in the past week, including that of a prominent lawmaker. "Organized crime is already at the core of our society, and the government is not wiling to

admit it," states a high-ranking police official who refused
to give his name."

Taken aback, Paola María stumbled upon a half-open
purse on the floor. Something in it caught her eye. Again,
the common sense of her left brain kicked in and she
reached for the phone. But her right brain immediately
took over and she let go. She opened the purse and pulled
out the object: a journal.

Ever careful to leave no print behind, she examined its
pages. She was fascinated by what she read. The notebook
was full of touching poems on only one subject: forbidden
love. She examined the cover and saw the name Amanda
written in filigree scroll. She again searched the purse
and found other similar notebooks.

Paola María simply could not stop reading, enthralled
by the verses. One of the poems titled "A Sigh" struck her.

Sublime emotions encaged in an illusion
that wishes to capture my gaze,
they only survive on your memory
to escape the imaginary maze.

Melancholy enveloped her as she realized that a seasoned journalist could choose her words both to condemn
injustice, and to move a reader. Paola María gave in to the
fatal mixture of weariness and resignation and hurried
to her bedroom, where vases full of fresh flowers, books,
and the notebooks with her own fictional writing awaited
her. She landed exhausted on her bed. In just seconds
she surrendered to sleep and dreamed that she was a
successful literary author.

Carmen Luisa tries to focus past the tears. She again
looks at her hands. Their nails are now devoid of all
nail polish and the only ring—the wedding band—is
now around a pinky finger, dancing at will. Her hands
are coarse, yet strikingly firm, enthusiastic, and agile.
"They seem overjoyed," Carmen Luisa thinks to herself,

"as overjoyed as a death-row prisoner who has been set free."

She opens a new document on the screen, then closes her eyes and counts to sixty. Her eyes open to find that nothing has changed. She is about to start her ritual finger count, when her hands join in impatient complicity and immediately begin to type in complete harmony. On the screen appear the words that for decades Carmen Luisa has been yearning to write:

"In Search of De La Trompa's Killer" and Other Detective Stories
By Carmen Luisa Nieves

She continues to write:

Armando Quiñones was the first officer able to identify the naked and skinned body found in the air twenty feet over Mexico City's largest dump site as that of Mexican tycoon Adolfo De La Trompa. Next to him was a journal, with a filigree scroll bearing the name of Amanda Reguero Fortuna, the television reporter who was found murdered that same morning in the home of another journalist.

The police tried in vain to seize De La Trompa's body and the journal, until the medium María Inés del Gorrión was summoned to the site. After whispering words that only the wind could understand, and casting to the breeze what appeared to be ashes, she was able to make the body descend slowly to the ground. The three policemen in charge of the investigation are puzzled over the fact that the journal is dripping blood that has no DNA whatsoever.

# ACHILLES' HEEL

*Pronto llegará, el día de mi suerte,*
*sé que antes de mi muerte,*
*seguro que mi suerte cambiará.*

With her favorite song in the background, Adela Marí abruptly reduces the speed of her white '67 Corvette as it cruises Los Mártires del Lunes Avenue. She wonders whether she will be able to swerve onto one of the side streets before the inevitable happens.

She curses the very seconds during which she was distracted by the guy at the bus stop. He was carrying a green canvas backpack filled with cans and bottles. At least that's what it looked like from ten feet away. Adela Marí needed to find a nearby store to buy milk for her two kids. Preoccupied with domestic thoughts, she forgot to time her cruise down the avenue. So now the inevitable is about to happen.

The silver Volvo in front of her shows no intention of speeding up, despite the fact that she has just honked her horn. The driver thrusts his arm out the window and flashes his middle finger. Only then does he speed

up. Seduced by the yellow traffic light, Adela María
speeds up just as the light turns red. Although her
intention was to go ahead, she must stop so as not to
hit the little old lady who is crossing at the very moment
the traffic light changes. She wonders whether it is
better to just run her over and avoid the unavoidable.

The pleasure she feels driving her collector car van-
ishes. When a traffic light turns red, Adela Marí always
has the urge to slow down and remain second, third,
fourth in line —any place except first. She now shuts her
eyes tightly, as if in pain. When she opens them, she finds
the driver to her right observing her pained grimace.

Adela Marí tries to control her shaking hands and
puts on her sunglasses, which, on her father's orders,
she seldom uses. "Successful women don't have to hide
behind sunglasses," he's told her.

She turns up the volume on the radio, and the roar-
ing reconstructed engine jerks to the rhythm of classic
salsa springing from the digital speakers.

Adela Marí makes an effort and listens carefully to
the music to quell her pounding heart.

"Damn the very moment I decided to ride by here,"
she tells herself, to make sure she hasn't lost her voice.

Although the air conditioner is on full blast, drops
of sweat slide down in a desperate pilgrimage from
her forehead and her armpits. She swears in silence
for not taking the precautionary measure of wearing
a shirt with sleeves or a stronger deodorant, for having
left her baseball cap in the trunk. The fit muscles she
has chiseled thanks to ballet and a personal trainer
are of no help; her pores continue to relentlessly exude
gallons of cowardice.

The truth is, Adela Marí does whatever it takes to avoid her current situation when traveling through the city in one of her cars. In her twenty-six years behind the wheel she has taken the time to calculate distances so that she never finds herself first in line behind a red traffic light. She has studied all sorts of maps of the city. She has obsessively gone over the continuous traffic-pattern studies made by analysts, learning how long it takes before a yellow light turns to red at any traffic light along her usual route. She knows by heart the sequences of each traffic light and knows how to avoid being stuck between a yellow and a red.

Her road manners are legendary; she'll let cars go by and even sacrifice punctuality as long as she is not the first in line behind a red light.

She is first in line now, though. With a quick calculation, she figures that there are forty-eight seconds left of suffering. The Smith & Wesson revolver hidden under the business magazines in the passenger seat offers, for the first time, little comfort. It has been her faithful companion ever since she was robbed, but it can do nothing to help her now that she is being robbed of her sense of order.

Adela Marí tries to remember how to cross herself. She thinks about calling Marcos, but changes her mind. By the time he answers the phone—which he usually leaves in the kitchen—the light will most certainly have turned green. She considers praying one of those long prayers her sister would recite when their aunt would come home drunk or high. Aunt Yoli had no job, no significant other, and no other choice but to take the children in when their mother —the perfect sister whom she had so hated—was killed by her own husband, their father.

Calling one of her closest employees made no sense, either. That would have compromised her well-earned moniker of the Tycoon of Barrio Ayunas. Singlehandedly, with little education, without parents, and with no other guiding power than her own volition, she had crafted a small business empire and dared anyone to question her leadership.

"Damn that old lady, damn the milk, damn the idiot who calibrated this traffic light," she mutters in a grimace, hoping it will help the trails of sweat evaporate on her body. "Goddammit!"

Only twelve seconds left for the threat to come knocking, tearing down her macho façade. For the second time in her life, she wets her panties and she can sense the humiliating stench of urine that comes from fear and from the two vodkas she'd had during the business luncheon. Her rearview mirror gives her a magnified look at the line of cars she must lead in the mission of speeding away, without hesitation, once the light turns green. She squeezes her eyes shut.

Adela Marí remembers the first time she felt weak. She was nineteen years old, and had to rush out of a class at the university to pick up Aunt Yoli at a dope dealer's six blocks from their home. In the car, her aunt berated her for being just as priggish and cowardly as her mother. Adela Marí was first in line behind what seemed to be an eternal red light. When it changed to green, she hesitated, and was unable to step on the gas pedal. She was paralyzed by her aunt's drug-induced diatribe and the incessant honking horns behind her.

Right then and there, she got out of the car and swore she would never suffer through another humiliation like that one.

Adela Marí opens her eyes. The blood-red light winks seductively at her and turns to green. Out of habit, she searches for the gas pedal with her right foot, but can't locate it. She feels the tiny tri-color butterfly tattooed on her jugular vein writhe as she makes the effort of moving her right foot. It's useless. She feels as if her foot is being held down by two concrete blocks. She tries to use her left foot, but it, too, is victim to her paralyzing fear.

The disharmonious orchestra of horns begins; in her despair she tries to reach down to press the pedal with her hand, but her usually faithful limb also disobeys her orders. Her mind is flooded with the cacophony of all the car horns in the city waiting for her, Adela Marí Rivera—a.k.a. The Tycoon of Barrio Ayunas—to finally take the decisive step that will allow them to go on with their lives.

Adela Marí makes a quick decision: she grabs the gun and gets out of the car. She turns around and looks at the line of cars all blaring their horns. She points her gun at them and laughs at how the noise suddenly dies down. She turns to the traffic light and needs only to pull the trigger once for it to break into pieces and cascade to the ground. A shot is fired from another car. Adela Marí stumbles. Before falling, before heaving her last sigh, she looks at the defiant flicker from the traffic light, which, like her, is left shattered on the cold pavement.

# THE CHALLENGE

If Renata de la Matta were to identify the object of her emotions, she would not hesitate to point to the engine she had reassembled.

She lets out a sigh. It's the only thing she can do after a hard but productive day in her workshop. She smiles as she contemplates her feat: reconstructing a Fiat 500 engine. It will no longer depend on the capricious whims of OPEC's oil prices. From now on, thanks to her determination her Fiat will run only on ethanol. Satisfied, Renata again looks around her mechanic shop, stroking the greasy tools and her stained clothes. She feels proud of what she has accomplished.

Renata had no idea that she would feel this way after putting the engine's last cylinder in place. It has been a while since she experienced this kind of pleasure. Physical ecstasy has always abounded in her life thanks to no shortage of lovers. She has had her share, learning early on to hide her intelligence and sardonic wit behind her well-formed physique, her abundant black tresses, and her perfect teeth—all thanks to her father's genes. But she still believes there is nothing more soothing than conquering the unknown. From experience she has learned that overcoming challenges opens the door to other sensations and adventures.

She gets up spryly, despite having spent so many hours sitting on her workshop floor. Had she been a smoker, this would have been the occasion to light up, kick back, and savor the moment. But Renata doesn't smoke; she never has. Seeing her father die of lung cancer and having an old boyfriend who was unable to smile without a nicotine fix were enough to keep her from ever trying even a puff. She swore that she would never be addicted to anything in order to enjoy life.

From a distance, she can hear the incessant ringing of her cell phone. She makes a mental list of who could be calling at that hour. It is too early for her daughter Mercedes to phone her from Australia. Maybe it is Leopoldo, the latest notch on her belt, calling to say he has gotten tickets to see their favorite Argentine rock band. Leopoldo would have to wait, because Renata is going to celebrate on her own terms.

She walks to the small office in her workshop and hangs the DO NOT ENTER sign on the doorknob. She enters, locks the door behind her, and is glad that the air conditioner is still on. The cool waves of air mingle with the streams of sweat flowing down her body. Slowly, the heat and weariness melt away.

Renata puts away her cell phone, disconnects her office phone, and shuts off her computer. She pulls out a bottle of white wine from her desktop refrigerator and serves herself a glass. With the remote control in her hand, she amps up the volume of her speaker system, and Ravel's "Bolero" fills the office. She dims the light and settles into the large leather chair that takes up nearly half of the room.

Renata closes her eyes and remembers the first time she heard that melody: she was sitting on one of the cane rocking chairs in her grandparents' home and Grandmother was scolding her, saying that the chairs were valuable and had been in the family for so many years. The hypnotic quality of that melody awoke in her the desire to some day use it as a backdrop for an important celebration.

Renata mellows out. She then begins one of her favorite rituals: going through each step just taken to attain yet another goal.

She analyzes how she's installed the engine's new intake and exhaust valves. *Exhaust*. Pronouncing that word takes her back to the very first time when she'd heard about fuel made from fermented corn. By then she was studying mechanics after years of teaching Latin American history. A fellow worker who had recently been to Brazil came back with stories about the first experiments with ethanol and its impact on exhaust valves.

Renata recalls the first time she became interested in auto mechanics: it was during her visits to her father's workshop. She remembers the smell of oil and gasoline, and the greasy parts that would later glisten after they were installed in the engines. It was enticing enough to pique her curiosity, and made her want to find out what made the engines her father worked on tick. Then, when she was back at her mother's home, greasy and reeking of oil, she was immediately rushed to the shower under the threat that she would never be allowed to visit her father again.

Since then, Renata has derived pleasure from challenging proscription. As a girl, she harbored ideas of following in her father's footsteps and becoming a mechanic. But fate—in the form of a handsome young suitor—and her excellent grades led her to college instead. Her desire to honor her mother's name and banish memories of the happy times amid sparkplugs and cylinders launched her toward newer challenges and she ultimately landed a Ph.D. in History. Her mother was so proud, more so since she was herself stuck in a menial government job and regretted having dropped out of college due to the unexpected pregnancy.

*Her mother.* She would always say that her family was her exhaust valve. *Valve.* Renata laughs inwardly at the fact that just hours ago, one of her greatest challenges ever was to install valves that could withstand greater compression. She made sure that the sparkplugs had the right heat range. *Sparkplug.* Her father nicknamed her Sparkplug because—he said—she was the spark that ignited his life.

Renata takes another sip of wine, pulls off her sneakers, and cuddles into her chair.

She feels excitement in the same way as when she is changing the ignition of her Fiat, or when, after her second divorce, she used up her savings to buy an auto workshop and quit her teaching career. They were small and great moments in her life. Her second husband was a historian from Spain whom she met while attending a conference on nineteenth century Latin American leaders. The memory of that first secretive encounter in a college bathroom in Barcelona relaxes her. She unabashedly slips her hand under her soiled shirt and touches her right breast. Her nipple responds generously and perks up.

Renata begins to feel pleasurable carburetion throughout her body, like the kind she felt when installing the new chrome pumps.

Ravel gives way to a catchy salsa tune. Renata moves to the rhythm of *Vagabundo y triste, solo yo he vivido, todo lo que tengo, yo lo he conseguido.*

She can't help but smile again at the way the song lyrics sum up her life: *Vagabond and sad, alone I have lived, all I have, I have attained it on my own.*

Her lips welcome another sip of wine. Her hand slides between her legs. The wine helps loosen her inhibitions and she is aroused by the thought of her Fiat's engine feeling that surprisingly wondrous sensation of ethanol traveling through it for the first time: tempting, promising, challenging. After a long hard gulp, Renata puts the glass down and her body gives in to the music that reverberates throughout the room.

She tries to push back thoughts about whether or not she has correctly installed the diaphragm pump. Her hands, however, continue their task, preparing her body for ignition. The rush of pleasure is ready to overtake her, but her discipline has always conspired with temptation.

She gets up, quickly undresses and rushes to the workshop. Renata turns on the Fiat's engine and lies down on the hood. The pulsating combustion through ethanol is smooth, and with a mixture of torment and delight, Renata moans. Thanks to the rumbling, nobody hears her.

She turns over on the hood, pleased, listening to Mozart's "Allegro," relishing the fact that the world is still at her feet.

# BLISS

The true measure of her success was not the ardent ovation from her colleagues, but rather the pounding in her chest. As a member of the European Commission, Anne Aimé Bergero, with fervor and conviction, defended her proposal on the commission's obligation to deal with the global economic crisis. Extending a loan to Greece for €80 billion had been a good start.

Anne was not the only delegate in favor of the measure, but her presentation had been the most convincing. One had only to look at the interpreters, moving their hands emphatically as they relayed her speech.

She defended the highlights of her proposal in her native French, which she had polished to perfection at L'Université Paris-Sorbonne. She switched to German when she saw the German commissioner nodding off. At times, she punctuated her speech with Latin, dissipating any questions regarding her education. She had, after all, made a name for herself working in a variety of European embassies.

Outside the room, shaking hands with colleagues, Anne glanced at her Hermes watch. Her whole being was begging for a break. She deserved it, she thought, because throughout these past months, she had been completely devoted to her work. What she needed now was some air and to go grocery shopping. Her pantry was screaming for something more than just cereal and packaged milk.

She headed through Rue Foissart toward Leopold Park. She began reminiscing about her earlier visits to Paris with her parents, who were diplomats that made sure their three children grew up to be citizens of the world. Anne's older brother became a heart surgeon and was working in Berlin; her young sister was a well-known professor of philosophy at Oxford.

Anne decided to follow in her parents' footsteps, empowered by the possibility of ending hunger, poverty and war. Even as a girl, she excelled in school, so no one gave it a second thought that she would some day become a high-profile political figure. At the age of nine she had received an award in her city of Neuilly-sur-Seine for raising 948 francs for a school of immigrant children. She raised the money by selling lemonade in the park —a professional even as a child— carefully adding and subtracting the money on the child-size cash register that had been her favorite toy since she was four.

Grown-ups found her endearing as she wore adult sunglasses while serving lemonade.

Anne looked at her watch again and was surprised to see the time. She turned around and walked to the nearest metro station. After a few seconds of thought, she decided to take the train to the Demey station to stop at her favorite supermarket, which always had fresh fruit and plenty of shoppers.

Throughout the ride, she laughed inwardly remembering the looks of surprise on the faces of colleagues. They knew that Anne had what it took, but never imagined her passion for the causes in which she believed. She couldn't wait to tell her husband, Antoine, about her day over supper and to check online for stories on her speech.

When she got to the store, she pulled out a list of items she needed for the week. Antoine, a diplomat at the UN, had already gone shopping the week before, but they still needed a few things for the twins' birthday party that evening; the girls were turning eleven.

Adroit at pinpointing the right verb or noun in several languages, Anne was even more so at skimming the supermarket aisles and picking up what she needed in the blink of an eye. Once she had gotten all of her items, she headed for the cash register.

As she waited in line, she carefully observed the cashier, whose jaws mechanically chomped on a stale piece of gum. The cashier picked up each item with indifference, using her acrylic nails, and did not flinch as she passed each object over the scanner.

Anne had always been captivated by that piece of technology screwed on to the conveyer belt, which would instantly transmit the price to a digital screen. What she found most enthralling was the peculiar sound the cash register made when the scanner could not pick up a price and the cashier would have to type in the numbers with her right index finger. The sound of 2.99 was very different from that of 4.95, Anne had discovered. More intriguing was the noticeable difference in sound between 3.97 and 3.99, despite the slight variance between the two figures.

She couldn't understand the cashier's frustration when the scanner didn't work and she had to type in the numbers manually. What was all the fuss about? Anne had always thought there was a certain magic to that hollow but meaningful sound. Besides, the cashier had an option in a crisis situation. This wasn't the case for people living in countries that were drowning in a cruel sea of debt. The Greeks of the world, Anne called them.

When Anne's turn came, her twelve items were scanned flawlessly, and the cashier smiled, knowing that her nails were not going to punch in any numbers this time. It was at that very moment that Anne's indignation surged to the point of near rage. Her cell phone started ringing, but Anne didn't care. Her goal at that moment was to remove each item from the bags into which the cashier had casually placed them. With the same passion that Anne engaged to help Greece climb out of its financial rut, she placed each item back on the conveyer belt and walked around to the cash register, where the cashier was taken aback. Anne pushed the startled cashier out of the way. She gingerly picked up each item and, refusing to wave it over the scanner, typed in each price: 2.79, 2.89, 3.49...

"These are magical sounds, empty but with a specific goal," Anne thought to herself. The figure 49 had the best sound; she made a mental note to tell the manager during the next staff meeting.

When she had finished with her own items, Anne began typing in the numbers for the next customer in line. The cashier finally snapped out of her stupor, and yelled out: "*Service!*"

Enjoying the flow of customers, Anne was still seduced by all the typing and felt, for the first time in many years, that her thoughts were in order. Any crisis could be solved by merely adding or subtracting a number, and without stepping on any egos. Numbers plus numbers, plus sales tax, equaled only numbers.

She was fascinated by the idea that at night she might only have to think about how a number plus another would equal a larger figure. No jobs would be lost, no homes would be foreclosed as a result of her work. She wouldn't lose sleep worrying over corrupt officials stealing government money, or thinking that the diplomat of X country would vote for the resolution presented by the diplomat of Y only because they had been to bed together the night before; or that the diplomat of Z would not vote for the resolution presented by the diplomat of R because he was upset over the cheap bottle of wine received as a New Year's gift.

"*Service des urgentes!*" cried the cashier.

Anne had already deftly typed the prices of eighteen items when the manager finally heeded the cashier's call. He looked puzzled at the new employee. Yet the customers were clearly impressed by Anne's unharnessed passion for typing each item and picking it up with such care, as if it were a Faberge egg. The manager walked over to Anne to speak to her, but she ignored him. The cashier, meanwhile, simply went home because she was done for the day, anyway.

Anne remained at the cash register with a disarming smile that only attracted more customers. Many left their places in other lines to queue up for Anne, even if that meant getting out of the store later. Her speed at typing numbers was incredible. Although the manager would stop by every fifteen minutes to check on Anne's sanity, he was already planning to propose to the supermarket's executives that they return to the old keypad registers.

After five hours of typing, Anne took her first break. She politely asked the customer to wait so that she could rush to the bathroom. She sprinted there and back before the manager came by to close cash register. It was midnight, but Anne would not budge.

"It's closing time," the manager explained. "Stop by tomorrow so that we can sign you up to work."

Anne looked at him as if he were crazy, and for a few seconds he actually thought he was. Three guards were summoned to remove Anne from the premises, but her threatening and furious gaze was enough to make them change their minds. Finally, all the supermarket employees left for the day, convinced that the woman would come to her senses at night when she was all alone.

Anne again heard the incessant ringing of her cell phone. She decided to answer, but at the same time she kept on typing to continue honing her skills.

"Anne, where the hell are you?" asked Antoine.

"At work."

"At this hour?"

"Yes."

The conversation went quiet until Anne resumed typing, fascinated by the sound made by the number 78.

"What's that I hear?" asked Antoine.

"The cash register."

"What cash register?"

"The one at the supermarket, which else?"

The cat was out of the bag. For the first time in many years, Antoine did not know what to say.

"Which supermarket?" he insisted

"The one where we always go."

At the crack of dawn the following morning, an online paper reported that a mob had gathered in front of the supermarket when Antoine arrived with three policemen. They had to wait for the manager to arrive at 6 a.m. When the doors were unlocked, Antoine ran inside and caught Anne sleeping on the conveyer belt by her cash register.

"Anne!" he cried.

Anne woke up. When she saw her husband and the police, she held onto her register.

There was no way to convince her that she was not a cashier and that she had a life outside the supermarket. She simply refused to leave. The supermarket's management decided to keep her there and hire a psychiatrist who, after several days of observation, concluded that Anne was simply sane. Besides, in the two weeks that Anne had been at the cash register, sales had gone up by 53.8 percent, fueled mostly by customers' curiosity over her passion for numbers, and thanks to her legendary politeness, her talent for handling each object with great care, as well as by the many news reports on the phenomenon. The supermarket's management even set up a small room with a shower for Anne and gave her seven sets of uniforms. Management instructed the cafeteria to feed her.

Antoine and the twins visited her from time to time. It seemed as if Anne did not recognize them, except when they were buying an item with a price that ended in the magical figure of 80, which reminded her of the financial predicament of Greece. It was only then that Anne would hear the melody of the typed numbers, look at them, smile, and wink.

# THE FORMULA

Seen from the stage, the few fans who are left resembled the remainder of an anthill recently decimated by a harsh insecticide. Linda, a.k.a La Güima, is watching from behind a burlap sack that acts as an impromptu stage curtain.

The ensuing ritual is all too familiar for La Güima after twenty-three years of leading the small band that livens up weddings, *quinceañeros*, graduation parties and town festivals. Despite her days on the road, her wide hips with tons of experience and thousands of memories, the video on YouTube with eighty-three hits, and a recording under an independent label, few people know La Güima. Critics slammed her only record—*The Tarantula in Your Life*—as an inconsequential production.

Bass player Joshua, the only member of Güima's Gang with a sense of piety, crosses himself. The other two women band members—Puruca, the keyboardist, and Jazmín on the sax—take turns for one last look in a cracked mirror. Puruca's highlighted locks are shiny as ever, her few wrinkles barely noticeable on her near-perfect and meticulously made-up face. The mirror, meanwhile, tells Jazmín that, three grandchildren later, she is still attractive.

La Güima has no need to gaze in the mirror, because she knows very well that looking back at her will be a fifty-something without even the slightest touch of makeup to cover lines etched by a life lived to the fullest, despite an unsuccessful singing career. Her ever-present smile displays an overbite of crooked teeth never tamed by orthodontics. That was how she got her childhood nickname of La Güima—the guinea pig—although she likes to think that, in life, she has been her own guinea pig, testing the boundaries of what might be thought ordinary.

The curtain rises. La Güima smiles with satisfaction at the clear sky. This time her band won't have to battle a downpour or the heat. The band members come out holding hands. Immersed in middle age, they want to prove that they still have what it takes to make music with an edge.

"Let's kick ass!" roars La Güima as she hits the stage, still holding hands with her bandmates. A high-pitched howl, rehearsed for years, gives way to the one-for-all-and-all-for-one ritual of holding hands.

"Yeah!" cries Mano, the drummer.

As if in a trance, the group envisions a magical transformation that is further encouraged by their tight, black leather outfits steadily stretched throughout the

years by the extra pounds. They close their eyes to forget
that the town square, which can normally pack thousands, has barely a hundred or so people that evening
for the city's fete. But singing and riffing on the guitar
are what really matter. La Güima wails, cries and belts
out the songs that she insists are heaven personified.

Filing through the city's stage earlier in the evening
as part of the celebration of the patron saint's festival
were a number of other performers: a clown, the *reggaetón* group, the salsa band, the merengue soloist, the
trio, and the digital music DJ. With votes in mind, the
town's mayor has covered all his bases by hiring acts
for all tastes. Güima's Gang caters to that tiny but loud
bunch that politicians like to call the "miscellaneous
crowd." The between-the-lines clause in the contract
demanded that La Güima include songs for left-wing-
ers, feminists, tree-huggers, and, of course, what Jazmín
calls the "outcasts of the earth." Güima's Gang is the
evening's closing act.

The night progresses smoothly, ensuring La Güima's
dream of being the revered queen of the stage. With
an aggressive guitar riff and her usual off-key delivery,
La Güima tunes out memories of the record company
executive who advised that she might become famous
one day if she took voice classes, softened her music,
lost a few pounds, put braces on her teeth, and stopped
dressing like a "lesbian". He also recommended that she
keep quiet about how she earned a living translating
school textbooks.

The act is about to end. There are about 30 people left
in the audience and La Güima's voice starts to break.
Someone requests "Sunstroke," a song by a Cuban

singer/songwriter who was denied a visa to perform in the United States. La Güima bows to the request and signals to the band with three fingers. The first chords are struck and the song filters through the audience, which remains unresponsive to the band's howls. Two groups of people make their way to the exit to fulfill their need to find some form of amusement elsewhere, in a less dismal atmosphere.

An audience member, already fed up with La Güima's discordant wailing, desperately searches in her bag and utters profanity for the organizers' idea of prohibiting beverages in glass bottles. She finds the only thing she can hurl at the stage: a pair of promotional sunglasses given out by a soda company during the *reggaetón* act. With all the fury in the world, she hurls the sunglasses at La Güima, who catches them in mid-air and puts them on, in the darkness of the night.

The shades mercifully hide a large portion of the singer's face, but she keeps pulling out chords punctuated by flats and heavily seasoned with pianissimos and fortissimos. La Güima hasn't changed her delivery at all, but there is something about her image in shades that begins to attract the audience: they suddenly see wonder, promise, power, mystery, talent. As if on cue, a wave of ecstasy envelops the public, which begins to move to the beat. They start hurling sunglasses at the stage. The other members of the band quickly scoop them up and put them on, following their leader. The band is reinvigorated with the audience's energy and responds in kind.

In minutes, the dozens swell to hundreds who are drawn to the fun. They couldn't care less whether the

songs are familiar, dated or had been played just minutes ago; the masked musicians had won the public over.

La Güima can't believe what is happening, but she
couldn't be happier, either. In one instance, she pulls off
her glasses to wipe the sweat from her wrinkled brow,
and was met with an eager: "No, keep 'em on!" from the
audience, which was by now convinced that the magic
would suddenly vanish if the musicians removed their
shades. Cries of "Encore! Encore! Encore!" followed.

Two hours later, the police, nightsticks in hand,
threatened to finally end the ongoing concert. They
had never seen such a huge audience at the festival.
They were finally able to subdue the crowd and escort
the band to its dilapidated bus.

***

Ever since that concert, no one would be able to look
at La Güima and her band members in the eye. The
group's hit "My Shades" won a Grammy after ranking
on the Billboard lists. The official Grammy pictures of
the Latin American winners showed La Güima proudly
posing in her sunglasses with her precious prize. Next
to her seven *reggaetón* singers and a jazz duo also pose
—all of them proudly wearing their signature mark:
oversized black sunglasses.

## ABOUT THE AUTHOR

*María Bird Picó* is a Puerto Rican journalist, writer and screenwriter. She has a master's degree in Creative Writing from Universidad del Sagrado Corazón, and another in Latin American Affairs from New York University. She was a Peace Corps Volunteer in Costa Rica in the 1980s and has been reporting for local and international publications for the past three decades. She made her debut as a writer in the 1990s when two of her short stories were published in *Te traigo un cuento*, an anthology printed by Editorial de la Universidad de Puerto Rico. Her novel, *El día que tu secreto se hizo mío*, garnered second place in the Instituto de Cultura Puertorriqueña's 2015 national literary awards in the youth category. Her first collection of short stories, *Tras esas gafas de sol*, was selected by literary critics of El Nuevo Día as one of the best local books in 2014. María is also the screenwriter of *La mecedora*, a short included in the *Voces de la mujer* film project produced by Puerto Rico's Film Commission. Aside from always wearing sunglasses, which she says shields her from other things besides the sun on her beloved Caribbean island, she loves to travel, read, binge watch movies and TV series, and spend time with her Tico husband, her two children and her dogs, Diva and Comay.

## ABOUT THE TRANSLATOR

*Melba Ferrer* has always lived and loved in two languages. She was born in New York and grew up in the Bronx and Puerto Rico. She obtained a bachelor's degree in modern languages and later a master's degree in translation, from her beloved University of Puerto Rico. For years, she worked as a journalist in both the Spanish and English media, until she embarked on a new life as a translator. She currently lives in San Juan, where she shares her tiny apartment with her husband, her son, her dog and her plants.

CPSIA information can be obtained
at www.ICGtesting.com
Printed in the USA
LVHW090556081019
633405LV00008B/3561/P